"What did you say to Madison to make her cry?"

Dominic's question, although whispered, was full of forceful steel. His taller frame towered over her smaller one.

Abbey straightened, her shoulders back. She had done nothing wrong. "We were talking about the dogs I have. She asked me if Gabe was the only one. I told her I also had two small ones. She mentioned she used to have a small dog named Zoe. She didn't exactly say it, but I assumed Zoe died in the plane crash."

A nerve jerked in his strong jawline. "I see," he clipped out, peering down the brightly colored corridor as emotions—first sadness, then anger, then something she couldn't read—flittered across his face. "She's gone through a lot lately." His murmured words, spoken so low Abbey barely heard him, held none of the forceful steel now.

In that moment, Abbey realized Dominic Winters was hurting as much as Madison.

Books by Margaret Daley

Love Inspired

*Gold in the Fire
*A Mother for Cindy
*Light in the Storm
 The Cinderella Plan
*When Dreams Come True
 Hearts on the Line
*Tidings of Joy
 Heart of the Amazon
†Once Upon a Family
†Heart of the Family
†Family Ever After
 A Texas Thanksgiving
†Second Chance Family
†Together for the Holidays
††Love Lessons
††Heart of a Cowboy
††A Daughter for Christmas
**His Holiday Family
**A Love Rekindled
**A Mom's New Start
§§Healing Hearts

Love Inspired Suspense

So Dark the Night
Vanished

Buried Secrets
Don't Look Back
Forsaken Canyon
What Sarah Saw
Poisoned Secrets
Cowboy Protector
Christmas Peril
 "Merry Mayhem"
§Christmas Bodyguard
 Trail of Lies
§Protecting Her Own
§Hidden in the Everglades
§Christmas Stalking
 Detection Mission
§Guarding the Witness

*The Ladies of
 Sweetwater Lake
†Fostered by Love
††Helping Hands
 Homeschooling
**A Town Called Hope
§Guardians, Inc.
§§Caring Canines

MARGARET DALEY

feels she has been blessed. She has been married more than thirty years to her husband, Mike, whom she met in college. He is a terrific support and her best friend. They have one son, Shaun. Margaret has been writing for many years and loves to tell a story. When she was a little girl, she would play with her dolls and make up stories about their lives. Now she writes these stories down. She especially enjoys weaving stories about families and how faith in God can sustain a person when things get tough. When she isn't writing, she is fortunate to be a teacher for students with special needs. Margaret has taught for more than twenty years and loves working with her students. She has also been a Special Olympics coach and has participated in many sports with her students.

Healing Hearts

Margaret Daley

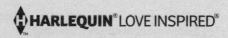
HARLEQUIN® LOVE INSPIRED®

Recycling programs for this product may not exist in your area.

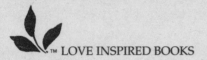

™ LOVE INSPIRED BOOKS

ISBN-13: 978-0-373-87830-7

HEALING HEARTS

Which is Christ in you, the hope of glory.
—*Colossians* 1:27

To: Vickie, Miralee and Kimberly—
thanks for the help

Chapter One

Abbey Harris climbed the stairs to the third floor at Cimarron City Hospital with Gabe, her black Lab, on a leash next to her. This was the only exercise she got all day. She worked long hours as a medical social worker at the hospital as well as volunteering to bring her dogs to see patients here to make them feel better.

At the door to the third floor, Abbey knelt and rubbed her Lab behind his ears. "Gabe, we've got a little girl who needs your love and care. Are you ready?"

He nudged her with his head, and she hugged him before standing and opening the door. The antiseptic smell and brightness from the fluorescent lights hit her as she stepped out onto the busy surgery floor in the middle of the day. A patient with a portable IV was strolling the hall, and she paused to let him pass.

When Abbey stopped at the nurse's station to check in with the head nurse on the floor, Gabe sat beside her. "Hi, Caron. I got your call about a patient you think Gabe can help."

Dressed in blue scrubs, Caron Wyatt looked up from reading a chart and smiled, her brown eyes twinkling.

"I'm so glad you and Gabe are here. If anyone can help, it'll be you and your dog. I've seen what you've done with other children on this floor."

"Which girl is it?"

"Madison Winters. She lost both her parents in a plane crash six months ago."

"I remember hearing about that. Greg and Susie Winters. What an awful story." Abbey patted the top of Gabe's head. She knew what it was like to lose someone close. She'd always miss her daughter, Lisa.

"Madison has come in for yet another operation. Hopefully it'll be her last one, and she'll be able to walk after it. That is, with physical therapy."

"Has she spent a lot of time in the hospital?"

Caron nodded, smoothing her short auburn hair back from her face. "Over the past few months I've seen the child grow more depressed, which really concerns me. You know how important a patient's attitude is to the recovery process."

"That's why I started bringing Gabe and my other dogs here to visit. It goes hand in hand with my job."

"I'm hoping he'll work his wonders with this little girl."

"Which room?"

"Three forty-five."

"How old is Madison?"

"Eight."

Abbey's breath caught for a moment before she released it. Her daughter, Lisa, would have been eight if she had lived. If only she hadn't died from leukemia… She couldn't go there now, not when someone needed to be cheered up. "We'll try our best."

When Abbey arrived at room 345, she stood in the

doorway to the little girl's hospital room, decorated in pink with purple accents and Disney characters painted on the walls. It was bright. Cheerful. Yet Madison sat in a wheelchair staring out the window with the saddest expression on her face.

Abbey tried to contain her emotions at the sight. She racked her brain, trying to recall what the reporter had said about the child and her situation. She had been the only survivor in the plane crash that killed her parents. Her half brother, Dominic Winters, had returned to Cimarron City to be with his little sister. Was he still here? Or was someone else looking after Madison?

Gabe nudged Abbey's hand as though he knew instinctively he could help the child. If any animal could comfort and cheer up Madison, her black Lab would.

Abbey took a deep, fortifying breath, then plastered a smile on her face and entered the hospital room. "Gabe, look who I found. Madison."

On cue, Gabe barked.

The girl glanced toward Abbey and her dog as they crossed the distance between them. The child's blue eyes grew round. "You were looking for me?" she murmured, her attention fixed on Gabe.

He stopped at the side of the wheelchair and sat, looking up at Madison. She was a fragile-looking child, with short brown hair and long dark lashes. For a few seconds she just stared at him.

"You can pet him. He loves kids."

"How did you get a dog in here?" Madison asked as she laid her hand on the top of Gabe's head. Tentative at first, she then began scratching him behind the ears.

"That's one of his favorite places to be rubbed. I'm Abbey, and he's Gabe." Abbey squatted down next to her dog. "I've been bringing him to visit different people in this hospital for a while now. I work here, and friends of mine let me know when there's someone special he should meet. One of them thought you might enjoy getting to know Gabe."

"Who?"

"Nurse Caron."

"She didn't say anything to me." Madison leaned more toward them, now using both hands to pet Gabe when he put his head on the arm of the chair.

"I told her I wanted to surprise you."

Madison grinned. "You did. I used to have a dog. A small one."

Abbey's heart swelled, thinking about what the little girl had gone through in the past few months. A picture of her late daughter hovered in her mind. She couldn't go there, or she wouldn't be able to cheer up Madison. She forced a light tone to her voice. "I have several dogs."

"You do? Are they like Gabe?"

"No, the others are smaller, what I would call lapdogs."

"Like Zoe was."

"Was she your dog?"

Madison nodded, tears welling in her eyes.

"What's wrong?"

Wet tracks coursed down the little girl's cheeks. "She was in the plane with me when it crashed. I tried holding on to her, but…" The last of the sentence ended on a sob.

Abbey ached at the sight of the child's tears for her dog. That piece of information hadn't been in the news reports she'd heard. She opened her mouth to say something comforting but a booming voice stopped her.

"What's going on in here?"

Abbey shot to her feet and whirled around to face a man over six feet tall with the same crystalline blue eyes and long black eyelashes as Madison. "I'm Abbey Harris, a social worker with the hospital. I bring Gabe here to see different patients. A nurse on the floor thought that Madison would enjoy meeting him."

As though she'd given him too much information to process, he stared at her with a blank expression for a few long seconds before turning his attention to Madison. "You're crying, Madi. What's wrong?" His voice softened as his intense gaze did.

The child swiped her hands across her cheeks. "Nothing. Gabe is a wonderful dog, Dominic."

So this was Dominic Winters, Madi's older brother. For a moment she thought of her ex-husband, who couldn't deal with his own child when she had been so sick. How very different these two men were.

He knelt by the wheelchair and held his hand out for Gabe to sniff. "I'm sure he is. I used to have a golden retriever when I was a boy."

Dominic Winters's commanding presence filled the room. He exuded power. Abbey couldn't imagine him as a child. Maybe because of all the stories she'd heard about him.

"Madison, I need to talk to Gabe's owner for a few minutes, then you'll be going down for some last-minute tests. Okay?"

"Can Gabe stay while you two talk?"

Dominic finally looked back at Abbey. "That's your call."

"He'd love to. You can have him do some tricks while I'm gone. Roll over. Sit. Shake hands. He loves to perform. I think he's a clown at heart," Abbey said, giving the young girl a wink right before she followed Dominic from the room.

The second she stepped outside into the hallway, she knew this wouldn't be a friendly little chat. He frowned as he moved a few feet from the doorway.

"What did you say to Madison to make her cry?" Though whispered, his question was full of forceful steel. His taller frame towered over her smaller one.

Abbey straightened, throwing her shoulders back. She had done nothing wrong. "We were talking about the dogs I have. She asked me if Gabe was the only one. I told her I also had two small ones. She mentioned she'd had a small dog. She didn't exactly say it, but I assumed Zoe died in the plane crash."

Dominic's jaw visibly tightened. "I see," he said between clenched teeth, peering down the brightly colored corridor as a myriad of emotions—first sadness, then anger, then something she couldn't read—flittered across his face. "She's gone through so much lately." His murmured words, spoken so low Abbey barely heard him, held none of the forceful steel now.

In that moment Abbey realized Dominic Winters was hurting as much as his younger sister. "I understand she'll have surgery tomorrow."

"Yes. It'll be her most difficult one to date, but I hope her last."

"I'd love to bring Gabe to see her during her recovery. He's helped a lot of patients, especially some who have been fighting pain and..." She held her tongue. It was only a guess from what she'd seen before going into the room.

"And what?"

Abbey doubted she would be telling him anything he didn't already know. "Before I came in, she looked so lost and sad. I know that depression can be an issue with people who are dealing with the kinds of injuries she has, not to mention the loss of her parents."

"Well, I *don't* think it would be a good idea to have Gabe visit her. I don't need her upset by anything. She's been dealing with so much."

"But—"

He started for his little sister's room. "Thank you for your concern, but we'll be fine."

The controlled politeness in his words, his stiff bearing, shouted the opposite. She hurried after him to retrieve Gabe, deciding that the man hadn't said anything specific about *her* not coming to see Madison. Remembering the loneliness she'd glimpsed in the child's eyes only strengthened her plan to help her as much as she could.

Good thing she worked at the hospital as a medical social worker. Dealing with families of patients was part of her job. Although bringing her dogs to the hospital wasn't technically part of her work, it helped when interacting with the patients and their families. As a child she'd learned the power of animals to help others when she'd assisted her father at his veterinary hospital.

Abbey spied her black Lab with his head lying in the girl's lap while she stroked him over and over. "I'm sorry, Madison, but Gabe has to leave. There are some other patients expecting to see him, too."

The child looked up at Abbey, that sadness dulling the color of her eyes. "Can't he stay a little longer?"

Abbey tossed a glance at Dominic. "I believe you

have some tests to do before your surgery. That's very important. You can't miss them."

Madison pouted. "The last two operations haven't helped. I don't know why I'm having another one. They don't even know if I'll walk again," she said in a fierce voice, then dropped her head, staring at Gabe, who scooted closer to her as though he sensed her emotional pain and wanted to help ease it.

Just like Gabe had done with Lisa. The memory intruded into her thoughts. She shoved it away again, the pain still raw.

"The doctor says you have a good chance of recovering the full use of your legs, Madi. It'll take lots of work and physical therapy, but I'll help you as much as I can."

The child leaned down and kissed the top of Gabe's head. "See you later, Gabe, then you can show me your tricks," she whispered in a thick tone.

The defeat in Madison's voice tore at Abbey. She peered at Dominic. His sharp gaze broadcasted that she needed to leave. As she called Gabe to come with her, she turned away, but not before she saw the man's grief. His eyes connected with hers, and he quickly veiled his expression.

"I'll be praying for you, Madison." Abbey rushed from the room, knowing she'd probably overstepped her boundaries. That wasn't wise considering Dominic Winters had the kind of power and money to make her life difficult.

At the nurse's station, Abbey stopped to see her friend. "Caron, thanks for the heads-up about Madison. Gabe and she hit it off right away, as you thought they would."

"When does Gabe not do that? Even Mr. Johnson

couldn't resist your dog's charm, and my nurses have never dealt with someone so grumpy. But Gabe got him to smile. I didn't think the man had it in him."

"You're exaggerating. Mr. Johnson has been in a lot of pain, but I think his meds are finally helping."

"Nope, it was definitely Gabe. Are you working tomorrow?"

Abbey nodded, her gaze straying back toward Madison's room. Dominic Winters, with a nurse's aide, wheeled his sister out into the hall and headed for the elevator. For just a few seconds his eyes captured hers, but he quickly averted them and bent down to say something to his sister.

"Yes. I'll be around. I want to make sure Madison's surgery goes all right. Mr. Winters may need my services."

One of Caron's eyebrows rose. "I don't see him needing anyone's services. Every time I've dealt with him, he knew exactly what he wanted."

That wasn't the man she'd gotten a brief glimpse of, but she could have been reading more into their encounter. "Maybe. He's probably anxious about Madison having another operation. Does that make three now in six months?"

"Yes. She had multiple fractures to both legs—a lot of damage to repair."

Abbey inwardly sighed. Her daughter, Lisa, had come to hate going to the hospital those last few months of her life. "I'd better go. Mr. Johnson is expecting Gabe."

"And we wouldn't want him to get upset," Caron said with a long sigh.

"No, we wouldn't."

Holding Gabe's leash, Abbey headed for the other side of the third floor, where the eighty-year-old man's room was located. The closer they got, the more Gabe pulled on the strap. The second she hit the doorway she unclipped Gabe, and he padded toward Mr. Johnson, his tail wagging frantically. The frail, hunched-over man sat in his wheelchair, his head down as though he had fallen asleep seated in front of the window. Tufts of gray hair lay at odd angles as though he hadn't combed it since he got up.

Gabe nudged Mr. Johnson's hand. He straightened, a grin spreading across his wrinkled face, an ashen cast to it. "It's about time you got here, boy. I expected you fifteen minutes ago." Mr. Johnson shot her a censuring look.

"Sorry about that. We paid another patient a visit before we came here."

"Are you going to come see me at the nursing home once I'm transferred?" His gruff voice wavered.

"Of course we are. I thought others at the place would enjoy meeting Gabe, too."

"Sure. Sure. So long as *you* come." Gabe perched his front legs on the arm of the wheelchair while Mr. Johnson rubbed him. "If I have to be in prison, I need something to look forward to."

"You can count on us. I talked to the Shady Oaks Nursing Home this morning. Everything will be ready." Another one of her duties at the hospital was often making arrangements for patients who were leaving for some kind of long-term care.

Mr. Johnson snorted. "That'll make my son happy. He won't have to deal with me."

"Now, Mr. Johnson, you know he cares about you. He comes to see you every night."

Another snort preceded a series of coughs. Tears crowded the old man's gray eyes. Gabe licked him on the cheek, and Mr. Johnson cackled as one tear slipped down his face. "He always knows what to do."

Abbey took a seat in a chair in a room decorated very differently from Madison's. The walls were pale blue with two generic landscape pictures. She watched as Mr. Johnson produced a ball he liked to toss for Gabe, one of her pet's favorite activities.

She used to throw a ball to Gabe for endless hours after her daughter's death because Lisa had loved to do that when she hadn't been too weak. If it hadn't been for her dogs, she didn't know if she could have pulled her life together, to finally finish her master's degree and become a medical social worker. But nine months ago, she finally did just that. She knew more than anyone the power of animals to heal a broken heart.

Later that evening while his sister slept, Dominic paced the hospital room. This was the last operation— at least he hoped so—the one the doctors said would give Madison a chance to regain her ability to walk. But there was no guarantee, thanks to the extensive damage to her legs. Each limb had multiple fractures from the plane wreck. When the rescuers had arrived on the scene, they had been surprised anyone had survived the crash. His father and second wife hadn't, along with Madi's beloved pet, Zoe. All the money in the world hadn't been able to bring his dad back, and it might not be able to give his sister the ability to walk or run.

His cell phone vibrated. He strode to the corridor to

answer the call. It was the one he'd been waiting for but dreading from the second in command of his clothing and textile company. "Yes, what's happening?"

"Not good, Dominic," Samuel Dearborn said, in a voice full of exhaustion that matched how Dominic felt. "Three of our employees were kidnapped. The rebels are demanding two hundred thousand each."

Dominic's stomach clenched. "We have to do whatever is necessary to get our people back. But this is it. I won't be threatened again and again. We're moving the factory back to the United States. We should have done that six months ago when the rebels grew stronger." But at that time his life had fallen apart, and his focus had been on burying his father and stepmother. Then he had to take care of his dad's business affairs, especially Winter Haven Ranch, as well as make sure his younger half sister got the care and medical treatment she needed.

"When will you be able to come back to Houston?"

"Don't know. I'm still needed here. Keep me updated." After Dominic hung up, he leaned back against the wall, the quiet in the hallway not the comfort he needed. But what would that be, exactly? His sister healed? Yes, but something else wasn't right.

Was it the situation in Costa Sierra? Maybe. He'd never been totally convinced that had been the best move for his company. The profit levels had gone up, but look at what he was dealing with now. He couldn't risk any more of his workers being taken for ransom.

His gaze fixed upon a scene painted on the wall across from him. A little white dog holding a ball in its mouth looking up at a boy. The dog reminded him of Zoe—the dog that had died in the plane crash, the one his sister had been crying about earlier when that woman—Abbey Harris—had visited with her black Lab.

For a few seconds an image of the social worker flashed into his mind. Her pert face, framed by medium-length chestnut-red hair, had held his attention, but what had kept him looking at her in the hallway were her eyes, looking like swirls of milk chocolate. Inviting. Full of concern. Could she and Gabe truly help his sister?

A scream pierced the air—a scream from Madi's room. Dominic raced inside and scooped his sister into his embrace while she lay in bed. "I'm here. You aren't alone."

Madi shook against him, sobbing and clinging to him. It had taken the rescuers twenty minutes to get to her in the plane wreck. She'd been there alone. Trapped.

The only thing that seemed to calm her was his re-assurances that she wasn't alone, that he was there for her. The few times he hadn't been, he'd gotten a frantic call from the housekeeper or a nurse at the hospital. That was why he always stayed in the room with her and hadn't yet returned to his life in Houston.

"I won't leave you, Madi," he whispered over and over until her cries subsided. "Ever."

She pushed her hair back, her eyes red, her face pale. "You weren't here."

"I'd only gone out into the hall for a minute." He sat back in the chair near the bed and held her hand. "Go back to sleep. I'll stay beside you. Nothing can hurt you now—not with me here."

She closed her eyes, but a minute later they popped opened, then slid shut again. Slowly her tense body relaxed. He kept holding her hand until he was sure she had fallen asleep. Tomorrow would be a long day with her surgery. He needed to get some rest, too.

He moved to the cot he'd been using and eased down onto it, his feet planted on the floor, his elbows on his thighs, his hands clasped together.

Heavenly Father, if someone has to suffer, make it me. I can't take seeing Madi go through this anymore. I've needed You these past months. Why are You so silent? I've gotten her the best doctors money can buy. It doesn't seem to be enough. What should I do?

The next morning, Abbey entered Harris Veterinary Hospital, which her father owned, and headed back to the examination rooms where he saw animals. Spying her dad writing something on a chart, she stopped, taking in the white lab coat he always wore at work. Distinguished-looking, with short salt-and-pepper hair, he was one of the kindest men she knew. Her childhood had been filled with animals and loving parents.

"Hi, Dad. Why did you want to see me? I can't stay long, or I'll be late for work." Abbey set down a cup of coffee from their favorite place on the counter for her father. "Who do you have here?"

"An abandoned dog. Someone left her on my doorstep this morning. She's in pretty good health and hasn't been on her own long. I wouldn't be surprised if her owner left her here."

She knew where this was going. At least once a month, they had this conversation. "I can't take another pet. I have three dogs and a couple of cats. With my crazy hours lately I feel I'm neglecting them." Abbey tried not to make eye contact with the white bichon frise with matted fur.

"I'm going to have to cut most of her fur off. She hasn't been brushed in a while, but she isn't too thin. She has fleas, but I'll take care of that as well as her shots," he rattled off as he checked the dog's ears, teeth, lungs and heart. "But I need a home for her." He fixed his dark eyes on her.

Abbey shook her head. "What part of 'I can't take her' do you not understand?"

"Oh, I heard you. But she's so sweet and loves to be held. Just ask around. She'll make someone a great pet. She could easily be trained as a therapy dog. Here, hold her while I give her a shot."

She started backing toward the door. "No, you don't. You think the second I hold her, I'll fall in love with her and take her. I know all of your tactics. Where's Emma? She's usually in here assisting you."

Her father ignored her protests and thrust the animal against her. "Emma's busy with another animal."

Abbey sighed, put her coffee down and took the quivering dog into her arms.

"She needs extra love right now." Her father finished with the shot and turned away rather than taking the bichon.

Just like Madison Winters. "You could always take her. Or Emma."

"I already have five dogs and two cats, besides taking care of this veterinary practice. And Emma took home the last stray."

"You already asked her, didn't you?"

He nodded. "I have to keep my assistant happy. She's

the best there is. Almost like having another veterinarian working here."

"I know." When Abbey made the mistake of looking down into the dog's brown eyes, she knew she was a goner. "Okay, okay. I'll try to find her a home. But no guarantees."

Her dad smiled. "Good. You can come pick her up after work today. Being at your house would be so much better than living in a cage here. Don't you agree?"

She laughed. "I could say no, but it wouldn't make any difference." Approaching her father, she kissed him on the cheek, then turned to leave. "Now I really do have to go. A little girl is having an operation, and I want to check on her this morning."

Abbey quickly left before her father found another animal for her to take home. In spite of her protests, she loved giving them a place to live. Along with the Lord, it was her dogs, especially Gabe, that had gotten her through Lisa's death and her husband's abandonment. But no pet could totally replace the emptiness in her heart.

Was that why she couldn't shake Dominic Winters and his sister from her mind last night? She'd even dreamed about the pair. And she'd relived the grief and pain in their expressions in that dream. She'd seen that in herself when her daughter had died—and it was still there locked deep inside her. Seeing Madison yesterday had brought it rushing back to the surface.

When she pulled into her parking space at the hospital, an idea started forming in her mind concerning the Winters family. She knew what might help Madison, and perhaps even her older brother. Abbey had promised her dad she would find a good home for the bichon frise. What if the abandoned animal could replace the dog Madison lost?

As she strode toward her office, she remembered Dominic's reaction to Gabe yesterday. Now all she had to do was convince him a pet would help Madison in her recovery.

Chapter Two

In the surgery waiting room, Dominic sat in a corner, spreading his work out on the small couch so no one would sit next to him. A crowd packed the area, taking every seat and making him unable to focus on the folder opened on his lap. The wall of people pressed in on him—had done so for several hours. But slowly, family and friends left when the nurse announced a patient's name.

Dominic scrubbed his hands down his face, his eyes stinging from lack of sleep. No matter how hard he'd tried to sleep last night, he couldn't forget what Madi would face today—a long operation that could make the difference in her life. He was also waiting for any news about his three employees in Costa Sierra.

Before his life had gone haywire six months ago, he would have flown to Costa Sierra personally to handle getting his people back safely. Although he felt he'd let his workers down, there was no way he could be in two places at once, and his sister needed him right now.

Dropping his head, he kneaded the tight cords of his neck. He'd stared at the same piece of paper for the past fifteen minutes and had only read a few paragraphs. He closed the folder, deciding he couldn't work with everything in turmoil. When he looked up, he caught sight of the woman who'd been in Madi's room yesterday with the dog. Abbey Harris. She saw him and grinned, then headed toward him. At least she didn't have the dog with her.

When Madi came back from her tests yesterday, she'd wanted to know where the black Lab was. He hadn't said anything because he still wasn't certain that having a dog around would help Madi heal. Losing Zoe had been so hard on her. In fact, she'd reacted more to Zoe's death than anything else, which concerned Dominic. His sister wasn't dealing well with her parents' deaths. He sometimes wondered if Madi thought her mom and dad would return from a long vacation. Even the counselor had remarked about Madi's silence when it came to her parents.

His gaze fixed on the lady dressed in bright yellow pants with a yellow-and-white shirt. Miss Sunshine flashed him a smile, which reached deep into her warm brown eyes. He slid his folder on top of his briefcase and rose.

"Hi, Mr. Winters, as I told you yesterday, I'm Abbey Harris and I work here as a social worker." She stuck her hand out.

As he shook it, he asked, "Is there something the hospital needs from me?"

"No. I just wanted to find out how Madison is doing. Have you heard anything about her surgery?"

"About twenty minutes ago a nurse told me everything is progressing the way it should."

Ms. Harris glanced around, spied an empty chair

nearby and dragged it closer, then sat. "I'd like to wait with you if that's okay."

He remained standing for a moment, not sure what to say to the woman.

She tilted her head back to look up at him. Her forehead scrunched, and she started to rise. "I'm sorry. I've intruded—"

He shook his head. "No, not at all." Taking his seat again, he continued. "I guess I haven't gotten past the part that you're a social worker. I hadn't had much to do with hospitals until Madi's accident. What do you do as a social worker at a hospital?"

"I specialize in medical issues. I often counsel patients, especially in connection with what's happening in their lives due to their health issues. I also oversee several support groups for patients and their family."

"Madi already has a counselor."

Abbey hooked a strand of hair behind her ear. "Another part of my job is to counsel families about what's going on with their loved ones. Health problems can have far-reaching effects on a person's family."

He stiffened, his fingers clutching the arm of the couch. "I don't need any counseling."

"You've misunderstood my visit today. I'm not here to drum up business. I'm merely here to find out how Madison is doing. She seemed upset when I saw her yesterday, and I brought Gabe in to help cheer her up."

"It didn't work. She was crying," Dominic said without censoring himself and regretted it almost instantly.

Especially when Ms. Harris's eyes darkened. She shoved to her feet. "I hope everything goes well. Madison is a sweet girl. Good day, Mr. Winters."

The frost that poured off the woman encased Dominic in remorse. Abbey Harris seemed so together, her life in control. He'd let his frustration about what was happening in his own life loose on her. And he deeply regretted it.

Abbey headed toward the hallway. The heat of embarrassment seared her cheeks. She should be used to being dismissed. More often than not, family members didn't want any help from a social worker.

When she left the waiting room, she increased her pace, wanting to put distance between her and Dominic Winters. She'd felt a connection with the man yesterday, having dealt with sorrow herself and been thrown into a situation she hadn't been prepared for. Her husband leaving her right before Lisa died had nearly destroyed Abbey. He hadn't been able to handle their daughter's illness and had sought comfort with another woman.

"Ms. Harris, wait."

She continued forward.

"Please."

She tamped down her burst of anger, stopped and swung around, coming face-to-face with Mr. Winters.

He closed the distance between them in the corridor. "I'm sorry. My worry over Madi's surgery isn't a good excuse for bad manners. Can we start over?"

For a split second, Abbey stayed angry. But his contrite tone soon melted her irritation. "Hi, I'm Abbey Harris." For the second time that day she stuck her hand out for him to shake.

He did. "I'm Dominic Winters. I appreciate your concern over Madi. Really."

His firm handshake reminded her what she'd read concerning him last night on the internet. A thirty-one year-old bachelor. He'd taken a small inheritance and built his company, Winters Clothing and Textiles, into a multimillion-dollar business in the ten years since he'd left Cimarron City.

When he released her hand, she missed the warmth of his touch. That caused her to look away, not sure where it had come from. She'd even dreamed about him last night—no doubt because she'd spent an hour surfing the web for tidbits about the man in hopes of finding something she could use to help convince him to let Gabe visit Madison.

"I was just feeling closed in back there in the waiting room. There must have been a record number of operations today. A good part of my time was spent on that small couch."

Abbey smiled knowingly. "I've got an idea. You can hang out in my office if you'd like." *Where had that come from?* "It's not far from here. I'll let surgery know that's where you are, and they can contact you there when Madison is in recovery. It'll be quiet. In fact, I've got tons of work to do, and it looks like you do, too." She couldn't believe she had offered her office. How much work would she really accomplish with him sitting only feet from her? He exuded strength and control—two characteristics that had served him well as CEO of a large company.

One corner of his mouth tipped up. "I've been attempting to do paperwork but not being very successful at it." He peered at the waiting room, then at her. "Are you sure?"

"Yes," she said, not as sure as she sounded. Her office was her retreat when her job got to be too much, but when she'd first entered the waiting room, she'd seen the expression on his face—a worried man in the midst of an uncomfortable situation. And she could relate to that.

"Let me get my briefcase." He darted back inside the room and returned half a minute later. "I brought work, thinking I would get some done. I've been going over the same report for an hour and probably couldn't tell you one thing concerning it."

Abbey headed for her office. She needed to see Mr. Johnson, who was leaving for a nursing home today, but she'd first get Dominic Winters settled. Mr. Johnson wouldn't be transferred until later this afternoon. "I found out the hard way trying to work at a time like this wasn't productive. During a difficult time in my life, I was in the middle of getting my master's degree, and trying to study was nearly impossible. I ended up postponing things till later. That was one of the best decisions I made during that time." She unlocked her door and entered.

"What happened?"

"My daughter had leukemia. The aggressive kind. Seven months after she was diagnosed, she died."

He stopped and stared at her. "I'm sorry."

"It was three years ago. Right after it happened, I thought I would never heal, but I am, slowly. I've used what I went through to help others. That's also when I learned how much an animal can help a person recover." Though she was used to talking about her past to patients and their families, it still brought up emotions that caused a lump in her throat. She swallowed hard. "I'm telling you this because I know what it's like to be in your shoes. It's tough being there for someone sick or injured and still trying to carry on with your life. One of the things that got me through was the support of my family and friends. And my pets, especially Gabe."

His eyes clouded. "I'm not married, and Madi is my only close family."

Abbey rubbed the finger on her left hand where her wedding ring used to be. She refused to think about her ex-husband. This wasn't about her, but Dominic and Madison. "I'm here if you need to talk."

He released a long breath. "I'm fine. Once Madi is out of surgery and on the road to recovery, life will settle down."

She'd told herself that, too, on the anniversary of Lisa's death. She'd hit the one-year mark, and in her mind everything would be all right after that. It wasn't. She'd received divorce papers a few days after the anniversary of her daughter's death, and finally had to acknowledge Peter wasn't coming back. That was only hammered home when her ex-husband remarried a week after the divorce was final. "I'll call Surgery and let them know where you are, and then I need to see a patient. Does Surgery have your cell number?"

"Yes." His gaze linked with hers.

The intensity in his look robbed her of words. Frantically she searched her mind for something appropriate to say. "Good. They can call you when Madison is going to Recovery."

While she placed the call, he took a seat on the couch in her office, setting the briefcase on the floor. Although she turned away from him, she was keenly aware of his movements, which sent a zing up her arm. Which shook her. She had no interest in dating, and yet her reaction to Dominic refuted that. She'd thought nothing could ever come between her and her husband. How naive she'd been.

When she finished talking to the person manning the desk in the Surgery waiting room, she looked toward him. "It's set up. Make yourself at home." She took in his dull gaze and the tired lines about his mouth. "Rest if you can. I'll be gone for a while."

"I think I will. Thanks." He leaned back, then closed his eyes.

Transfixed by his long dark lashes, Abbey stared at him as she fumbled for the door handle. Yes, he was a handsome man. Commanding. But so was her ex-husband and look at what had happened.

Abbey hurried into the hallway toward the elevator. She always tried to help patients and their families as much as she could, but there was something about Dominic Winters that made her want to go above and beyond. He seemed lost, and she wasn't even sure he realized it.

As she approached Mr. Johnson's room, she planted a smile on her face. Without Gabe, she would have to work harder to cheer up Mr. Johnson, who was fighting this move to the nursing home even though he couldn't take care of his own needs right now. With no family nearby interested in helping out, he had few options, and he'd finally recognized that.

"Mr. Johnson—" Abbey entered the room and came to a halt. It was empty, all signs that Mr. Johnson had been in it gone. She checked her watch and noted the time. Ten o'clock. Shady Oaks wasn't supposed to pick him up until two.

Had he died? For a few seconds, her heart pounded

against her rib cage, and she hurried to the nurse's station. They always notified her when someone passed away.

"Where's Mr. Johnson?"

The nurse's eyes grew wide. "Oh, no. I had a note to call you and forgot. Shady Oaks came early."

Abbey sighed and leaned against the counter. "I thought something…"

"I'm sorry. He wasn't too happy, but he went."

"I was going to have a late lunch and bring Gabe to give him a send-off."

"It's been crazy around here. A couple of emergency surgeries have been keeping us hopping."

"Anything I can help with?"

"No, we've got it under control now."

"Don't worry. I'll go see Mr. Johnson after work."

As she headed toward the elevator, concern for the older gentleman took hold. He didn't like change and the nursing home coming early to pick him up no doubt had thrown him off. Abbey could only imagine how angry he'd been. Technically he wasn't her problem anymore, but she couldn't just turn her back on the man. He was alone and in need of help—just like Dominic Winters. And neither man knew how to ask for help.

Dominic's cell phone rang. He jerked awake, sitting straight up on the couch in Ms. Harris's office. He blinked, orientating himself to his surroundings as he fumbled for the phone in his pocket.

"Yes," he said without looking to see who called.

"Dominic, this is Samuel. I wanted to give you an update on what's happening with the negotiations with the rebels. We offered to pay the ransom but haven't heard anything back from them."

"That seems odd. They're getting what they want." Acid burned in Dominic's stomach. He would do anything to protect his people, but he hated giving in to the rebels.

"I know, and the Costa Sierra government isn't quite sure what's going on. I'll let you know when we hear from the rebels, then I'll make the arrangements for the exchange. You're not to worry about it."

"I know everything is in good hands with you, but I'll worry until the three employees are home safe."

"Has Madi had her operation yet?"

"She's still in surgery but—" he glanced at his watch "—she should be through soon." If all went well. That point rattled around in his thoughts, and he missed what Samuel said next.

"Dominic, are you all right?" Samuel said, an urgency to his voice.

"Yes. My mind has been elsewhere. Call me when you know what's going on in Costa Sierra."

He placed his cell phone on the couch next to him and leaned back, wondering what he would do if the operation didn't really fix Madi's legs. He was ill equipped to deal with this situation. He'd wanted to be a father years ago. He'd even thought he had found the perfect woman to marry and start a family with. Then he'd made the mistake of bringing her home to the ranch to meet his father. Six months later she'd married his father and a year later Madi had been born. He loved his sister, but he'd had a hard time letting go of what Susie and his dad had done to him. His father had been grooming him to take over Winter Haven Ranch at the same time he was moving in on his fiancée. It was after that that Dominic had left Oklahoma and headed to Houston.

Now, after ten years of hard work, his company was finally what he had always envisioned it to be. He hadn't depended on his father for anything. When Dominic had taken his inheritance from his maternal grandparents and started Winters Clothing and Textiles, he had broken all ties with his father and stepmother. But it was little Madi who brought him back to the ranch occasionally.

When the door opened, Ms. Harris entered and looked at him, concern dulling her brown eyes. "Is something wrong with Madison?"

He schooled his features into a neutral expression, not used to sharing himself with others, even a beautiful woman who had allowed him the use of her office. "No. I haven't heard anything yet. I was just thinking."

"Everything okay?"

He must be losing his touch. He usually could prevent his emotions from appearing on his face. That ability had served him well in the business world. But for the past six months nothing had been the same for him. And he was discovering Abbey Harris was quite perceptive, which was an asset as a social worker. "Problems with a work situation," he said when he realized she'd moved closer, concern growing in her eyes.

"Your three missing employees in Costa Sierra?"

"How do you know about that? They were supposed to keep it quiet."

"It's all over the internet this morning."

"Great. I really shouldn't be surprised." Why hadn't Samuel told him? Probably trying to protect him while he was dealing with his sister's surgery. He would let his second in command know that he wasn't fragile. He needed to be aware of everything. That was the problem. He wasn't doing his job adequately, and he wasn't being a brother to Madi adequately, either. He didn't tolerate failure in anyone, least of all himself, and right now he was letting everyone down.

"Sometimes when life comes crashing down around you, you have to step back and regroup. Don't be afraid to ask for help. Do you have someone handling the situation in Costa Sierra?"

That was his problem. He had a difficult time asking anyone for help—even the Lord. When all his plans with Susie had fallen apart years ago, he'd worked hard to make sure he never had to suffer through that kind of pain again. And yet he had—with the death of his dad and Susie. "Yes, my second in command is handling it," he answered when he again realized she was waiting for a response.

"Then let him."

"It's *my* company, *my* employees."

"What about your sister? If the operation is successful, she'll be having intense physical therapy and will need someone there to cheer her on. It'll be a long road for her until she walks again. And if the surgery isn't successful, you'll have a whole other set of problems, teaching her to deal with living in a wheelchair."

"You sure know how to cheer me up."

"I don't take you as a guy who avoids problems. I have a feeling you like to meet a challenge head-on."

That was a good description of how he operated—until his father died suddenly of a heart attack while flying his plane and left him guardian of his younger, injured sister, who seemed to need more than he could give her. He'd buried so many of his emotions years ago that he was struggling to give her what she needed.

His cell phone sounded again, and he scooped it off the cushion, this time noting it was the hospital calling. "Yes?"

"Madi has been taken to Recovery. The operation went well. You'll be able to go back there in about fifteen minutes to see her. The doctor will stop by and talk to you then."

"Thanks. I'll be there." He rose and stuffed his phone in his pocket, then bent over to pick up his briefcase.

"Is Madison out of surgery?"

He peered at Abbey with her red hair hooked behind her ears, small gold studs in them. His gaze shifted to her face. She was neither smiling nor frowning as he looked into those eyes of hers. Big. Expressive. And full of concern that he wouldn't let himself respond to. He didn't need any more complications in an already complicated life. "Yes, she's being taken to Recovery."

"How did she do?" Abbey took a step toward him. Then another.

Trapped by the warmth in her gaze, he remained still, the space narrowing between them. "Good, I think. I'll know more when I talk with the doctor."

Silence fell between them. He needed to leave and yet… He clenched his briefcase tighter. "How was your patient?"

"Gone," she said, then quickly added, "Not dead, but he left earlier than expected for the nursing home."

"I'm glad he's all right." Dominic backed away. "Thanks for allowing me to sit in your office. I even managed to catch a catnap."

"Good. Rest can be one of the hardest things to get in a crisis."

"I don't think I've had a good night's sleep for the past six months. I'll never take it for granted ever again."

"I've been there. I know what you mean, Mr. Winters."

With another step, Dominic encountered the door. She did understand. "Please call me Dominic. After all, you shared your office with me, and I appreciate that, Abbey."

She smiled, her brown eyes shining. "Tell Madison I'll come by and see her soon."

He remembered his sister's comments about Abbey's dog last night. "Would you bring Gabe with you?"

Her grin widened. "If you want me to, I will."

"Yes, I was wrong yesterday. Madi enjoyed seeing Gabe. She hasn't talked much about losing her dog. In fact, she hasn't said much about losing her parents. Not even to the counselor. So mentioning it to you was a good thing, even with the tears."

"I'm glad she did."

The gleam in her eyes turned them to a cinnamon shade that made Dominic want to see close up. But he quickly abandoned that notion. "I'd better be going. I want to be there when she wakes up."

Abbey moved toward him. "I'm taking Gabe to see the patient who went to a nursing home today. After I see him, I'll bring Gabe by for a short visit when she's out of Recovery. If it goes well, I can bring him back again. That is, if it's okay with you."

"Let's see how it goes. This is all new for me, and I have to admit I'm struggling with my new role in Madi's life. I knew how to be a big brother, even a long-distance one, but this…" As the words spilled from his mouth, surprise flitted through him. Through the years, he'd worked to present a tough facade in a cutthroat business world. To admit he didn't have all the answers seemed so strange, but it was true. He needed help. After six months, he could finally admit he was totally in over his head, and barely treading water.

"You're still her big brother, too. When they become parents, most people have to learn as they go. Raising children is predictable at times but also very unpredictable. That's what keeps it interesting, as well as…" Abbey's voice faded.

She averted her eyes, but not before he saw a sheen to her eyes. Was she thinking about her own daughter? "You okay?"

She cleared her throat. "Yes." The corners of her mouth hitched up for a few seconds but didn't stay. "You'd better get a move on it. I'll see you two later." She leaned around him and opened the door.

Her scent—like a bouquet of flowers—wafted to him. He drew in a deep breath, thinking about a special place on the ranch in the spring where the wildflowers grew abundantly and filled the air with their aroma. Since returning, he hadn't had time to ride as he used to. He missed that.

"Bye," he murmured, and walked into the hall. He felt her gaze on him and glanced back. A connection arced between them. They both had lost someone important in their lives. With a nod, he continued his trek toward the recovery room. He knew how hard it was for him to lose a father—even one who had betrayed him. He couldn't imagine how awful it would be to lose a child.

Abbey rested against her door, desperately fighting to hold back the tears. Normally she was fine, except at odd moments when she felt overcome with her grief. She had so much to be thankful for. The Lord had given her a new direction, helping others rather than pitying herself. She had to focus on that, or she would let her sorrow overwhelm her again. But with Dominic, she felt his loss, too. And she felt something else—an attraction.

I can't go through that again.

Chapter Three

"**I** thought you forgot me," Mr. Johnson said the second Abbey came into his room at Shady Oaks Nursing Home later that day.

"I'd never forget you. I didn't know they were moving you earlier than planned."

Gabe tugged on his leash and dragged her toward the older man sitting in a chair positioned by the window that overlooked a garden bursting with the bright colors of summer. She let go, and Gabe made a beeline for Mr. Johnson, who greeted him as if he hadn't seen him in days.

"Neither did I. I told them they couldn't operate like that. People need to plan for changes."

"If only that could be the case every time."

He chuckled as he stroked Gabe's fur. "Yeah. It would make my life much better." When he patted the arm of his wheelchair, her dog propped himself against it so Mr. Johnson could hug him. "I sure missed this, boy. I didn't know what I was missing not having a dog for all these years."

Watching the man's face glow with contentment

made her heart fill with joy. "You know I could check with the nursing home and see if they allow pets for the residents. I have an abandoned dog left at my father's veterinary clinic that needs a home."

"What kind?"

"A bichon frise. She's about this tall." She indicated a few inches over a foot. "Pure white with a curly tail."

Mr. Johnson shook his head. "Nope. I want a manly dog. Like Gabe. He's perfect for me." He rubbed his face along Gabe's neck.

"I'll be on the lookout for one, but first I need to see if you can even have a pet." She couldn't give Gabe away. He was a part of her family, had been there for her through the good times and bad, but maybe she could find a similar dog for Mr. Johnson. As her dad had pointed out, people left animals on his doorstep for him to take care of because he was a vet, so it wouldn't be too long before another one turned up at the animal hospital. "Before I leave, I'll see if the director is here."

"The old battle-ax." Mr. Johnson snorted. "Forget it. She won't allow anything to disrupt how Shady Oaks is run."

"And you know this after being here less than half a day?"

"Yes. I saw and heard things at lunch. She runs a tight ship." He tapped his temple. "Not much gets past this steel trap. I may have lost the ability to walk, but my mind is sharp as a tack."

"Keeping things running smoothly can be a good thing. You know what to expect."

"You're right. I expect her to say no." As he patted Gabe, he continued, "Did I ever tell you about that time in the navy when we snuck a couple of cats aboard our ship to rid it of the mice and rat problem?"

"No." Abbey took a chair across from Mr. Johnson so she could listen to one of his many stories.

When Mr. Johnson finished telling her his escapade that landed him in the brig, he yawned. "I can't believe my own story almost put me to sleep. You're a jewel to listen to this old man."

"I told you I was a good listener. But I still have a young lady to take Gabe to see."

"I have a rival for his affections?"

"Yep, she's eight years old and had surgery today. She needs some cheering up."

Mr. Johnson took Gabe's head in his hands and said, "You hear that? You go make that child happy and tell me about it when you visit again." He peered up. "You two will come again?"

"Just try to keep me away. Tomorrow after work."

On her way out of the nursing home, she stopped by the main office and asked to speak with the director, Mrs. Rosen. When Abbey greeted the fortysomething woman, her mouth pinched together and she pointed at her dog.

"How did you get him in here? We have a rule about no animals in the building."

She should have checked beforehand, but so many nursing homes allowed them inside. "Pets are wonderful therapy for people who are lonely and depressed. It would be nice to bring some small pets in."

"No way. Not. Possible," Mrs. Rosen said. "Our patients aren't lonely. And pets can be so disruptive. I have a full staff that engages the people on their ward whenever they can. They don't have time to take care of animals on top of patients."

"I brought Gabe to cheer up Mr. Johnson. This move has been hard on him. I take care of my dog, so the staff doesn't have to. Mr. Johnson expects me to come tomorrow with Gabe. Do you have a problem with that?" How could this woman not see how good animals were for people?

"That's fine so long as you and he meet out in the courtyard. Animals belong outside, not in here, even for a visit."

Her blood starting to boil, Abbey counted to ten before she responded to the manager. "Do you know who I am?"

The lady arched a brow. "Abbey Harris, according to my secretary."

"I'm the social worker at Cimarron City Hospital. I often have to place people in nursing homes when their hospital insurance runs out, but they still need care. From the literature I've read an animal can calm a patient otherwise agitated, lower a person's blood pressure. I can run off some copies of those articles for you to look at."

"That's okay. That still doesn't address the care it would take if individual patients had their own pets. Like I said, not possible. This place would become a kennel, not a nursing home."

Anger festered in the pit of Abbey's stomach. Mrs. Rosen wasn't even willing to check into the benefits of animal therapy and make some concessions. "If this home isn't friendly toward its patients, I'll have to consider others in town."

"I'm a good friend with the director of the hospital. Mr. Hansen won't be happy to hear about your threat."

"It's part of my job to offer the best options to our patients, which include animal therapy. According to Mr. Hansen, the patients come first. Good day, Mrs. Rosen." Abbey hurried from the woman's office before she made the situation worse.

Abbey had let her anger get the better of her. Indeed, Mrs. Rosen might have more influence with Mr. Hansen than she did. She'd been working at the hospital for less than a year and had hardly seen the man who ran the place. But she did believe strongly in the power of animals to help people and speed the healing process along.

Somehow she would change Mrs. Rosen's mind, so Mr. Johnson could have a pet or at the very least regular visits from Gabe inside, where the heat of summer wouldn't be an issue. In a few weeks the temperature could be in the hundreds. Once Gabe had started visiting him on a regular basis, it had transformed an angry man into an affable one.

Twenty minutes later she pulled into the hospital parking lot and strolled toward the back entrance. Using the stairs, she and Gabe climbed them to the floor where Madison's room was. Before she'd left for the day she'd checked to make sure the little girl was back in her own room. Caron had told her Madison was doing great, more awake and alert than after her previous two operations.

She knocked on the door and waited to hear "come in" before she entered.

Dominic stood on the opposite side of the bed from Abbey. "She's been sleeping awhile now. I'll tell her you and Gabe came when she wakes up. Maybe you can come back another day."

"We can stay awhile, if that's okay with you. I don't have anything special to do other than pick up a new dog Dad wants me to take."

"How many will that make?"

The sight of his smile, which quirked the corners of his mouth, fluttered her stomach. "My fourth one. I'll have to apply for a kennel license if I get too many more. This particular dog was left on the doorstep of my dad's clinic."

"He's a vet?"

Tired after a long day, Abbey came around the bed and sat on the couch. Gabe stretched out on the floor at her feet. "Yes, and I'm the first person he tries to pawn any abandoned animal off on. I've had to put my foot down a number of times or that would be my full-time job." She grinned when she thought of her dogs greeting her when she came home from work. "Actually that wouldn't be too bad a job. It just wouldn't pay anything for me to live on."

Dominic scooted his chair around to face her. "I used to have a horse when I lived at the ranch, and Lightning had a dog that shared his stall with him. Dusty was a mutt that wandered into the barn one day and never left. My dad was a sucker for a stray animal. Used to drive my mom crazy. After she died, Dad stopped adopting animals. I asked him one day why. He told me her death took all the fun out of trying to find a way to have one more pet."

Abbey chuckled. "That kind of sounds like my parents. The problem is my mother is a cat person and my dad a dog person. That's caused a few arguments through the years."

"You took after your dad then?"

"Not really. I have two cats, too. I won't be surprised if Mom tries to give me another cat to try to even out the numbers some."

"It sounds like you have a zoo at your house."

"I grew up with animals all around me and loved to help Dad at his veterinary hospital."

"Why didn't you become a veterinarian like your father?"

She let out a long breath. "That was a bone of contention with my dad. He thought I would and didn't understand why I wouldn't. He didn't count on the fact I loved animals so much I couldn't deal with seeing them hurt all the time. I don't know how he does it day in and day out."

Dominic looked away, a frown carving deep lines in his face. "Sometimes what our fathers want isn't what's good for us."

Abbey wanted to ask him what he meant by that last statement, but an expression descended on his face that stopped her. Anger? Hurt? She wasn't sure, but she did know one thing—Dominic didn't want to talk about it. She searched her mind for something else to talk about. "I think I might be banned from Shady Oaks Nursing Home after today. I let my temper get the better of me."

"What happened? Did that involve the patient who moved to the nursing home?"

Abbey related her conversations with Mr. Johnson and Mrs. Rosen. "My impulse is to bring a ton of articles on animal therapy to the lady and dump them on her neat, well-organized desk, but I suppose she wouldn't appreciate that." Abbey smiled. "I might mess up her routine and that is not allowed. I don't think the woman is an animal lover."

Dominic's laughter echoed through the room. She liked hearing it. Rich and deep. The corners of his eyes crinkled and dimples appeared on each of his cheeks.

"Maybe I should teach you the art of negotiation," he said when he finished laughing.

"I'll have you know I'm usually quite good at it. I even know how to compromise. She just riled me today."

"What are you going to do about Mrs. Rosen?"

"Win her over, somehow."

"I have a feeling you'll succeed."

His declaration sent goose bumps flashing up her arms, and she felt a blush heat her cheeks.

"I think I see some bulldog characteristics in you."

Abbey burst out laughing. "I'm trying hard not to take offense. I'd rather believe you meant I'm simply a determined person."

His gaze riveted to Abbey. Intense. Probing. Assessing. For the life of her she couldn't look away. In that moment a connection sparked the air between them, heightening her senses to the man struggling to help his sister.

"In the short time we've known each other, that's one of the things I've learned I like about you. You know what you want and go for it. I won't be surprised if Shady Oaks has more than one dog there before this is over. And I agree, taking care of an animal can be good for a person."

"It can turn their focus to something other than their problems. There are two wings that have patients who only need assisted living. They should at least have an opportunity to have a pet if they want." She finally dragged her gaze from Dominic and noticed Madison stir in the bed. Abbey gestured toward the girl. "She may be waking up."

By the time Dominic turned around to face his sister, Madison's eyes eased open, and she spied Gabe. "You brought him." She smiled.

Abbey pushed to her feet and covered the distance to the bed. "There is no way I would disappoint you. Besides, Gabe was excited to come up here to see you. Weren't you, boy?"

Her dog barked, his tail wagging.

Madison's grin widened. "I'm glad."

"We won't be able to stay long, but we'll be back tomorrow. Gabe wants to make sure you're getting better. He loves to listen about your day."

"He does?"

"That's one of his gifts. When my daughter was sick, he was there for her every day."

"You have a daughter?"

Abbey pushed her sorrow down so she could answer the child. "Yes, but she went home to be with the Lord."

"Like Mom and Dad." Madison's eyes misted, and her smile drooped.

"Yes." Abbey cupped her hand over the girl's. "So remember Gabe's gift. He's special."

"I will." Her eyelids began to slide close. "Thirsty."

Since Abbey was closer than Dominic to the water pitcher, she poured some water into a pink plastic cup and helped Madison sit up enough to sip out of a straw. "How are you doing?"

"O-kay." Madison sank back on the bed and drifted off to sleep again.

Dominic stood beside Abbey. "Even when I know she's in pain, she doesn't say much. I worry she's holding it all inside, especially about her parents, and it's building up. She doesn't even talk much with her counselor, and they've been together for months."

"How someone copes with trauma varies from person to person. If you'll be okay with it, I can have Gabe visit every day, and we can leave them alone some. She may talk to him when she won't to a person. I found that worked with my daughter. Even at five, Lisa was trying to be brave for me. But once, when I had to leave the room for a few minutes, I heard her talking to Gabe. I found out how she was really feeling, and it helped me to help her."

"I'm willing to try anything. I want my sister well and able to be a child again."

"How long is she going to be in the hospital this time?"

"A week. It'll depend on her pain level and her progress after the surgery."

"Then tomorrow I'll bring Gabe by at the end of my day. I can go home to get him and bring him back. I usually make the rounds with him to certain patients a couple of times a week. Are you staying here all the time?"

"Yes, except when the housekeeper can relieve me for a little while. She doesn't like hospitals and prefers not to come by very much."

So it was just him taking care of Madison. Alone. At least with Lisa, Abbey's mom and dad had come to help her whenever she needed them. "When I come, I can give you some time to yourself. I know how important that can be. Go home. Take a shower. See to things you've let go."

He looked at Madison. So did Abbey. Madison's dark eyelashes were in stark contrast to the pale cast of her skin—as though the child had spent months indoors, which was most likely the case with all her injuries.

"I need some coffee. I'll walk you out," Dominic said, weariness in his voice.

As he started for the door, Abbey hung back for a few seconds. She'd barreled into this man's life. She didn't blame him for backing off. When she saw a need or problem, she went in and tried to fix it. She'd had to do so much of that when dealing with Lisa, then her husband's abandonment, that it had become second nature to her.

Out in the hallway, she paused, forcing Dominic to stop and look at her. "I'm sorry. I can come on too strong. I don't mean to take over, but I've been through what you're going through and was trying to use that knowledge to help you and Madison. I'll understand if you don't want to do what I suggested."

"You will? Remember I know about your bulldog tendencies." His mouth turned up into a half smile. "Actually your suggestions make sense. I can't help Madi if I'm so tired I can't string words into a coherent sentence. I could use a break. I didn't want her to hear me say that. I don't want her to think I don't love her. I do. From the day she was born. But at the same time, I've let my other responsibilities go. I have over a thousand employees who depend on me and my company for their livelihood. I've been thankful I have a good CFO, but I still need to oversee some issues."

"Like the rescue of your kidnapped workers?"

He closed his eyes for a second. "Yes. And there's still no word on that, which concerns me."

"Then let me help."

"Why? Until yesterday we were strangers."

"Because I can. Because…" No words came to her mind. How did she explain she felt deep down she should help? "Like I said, I see a need and jump in with both feet."

"No matter how deep the water is?"

She pictured herself on top of a high cliff, getting ready to leap into a roiling sea far below. "You forget I've been in this water before. I had my parents and cousins to help me. It sounds like you've got a reluctant housekeeper and no one else."

He glanced at her left hand. "Not your husband? I've noticed you aren't wearing a wedding ring."

The thought that he'd checked sent another blush to her cheeks. "No. We're divorced."

"I haven't lived here in over ten years, and what family I have is distant and scattered all over the country. My friends are in Houston, and since I've been back, I haven't had a chance to renew old friendships."

He was alone. How could she turn away? "Tell you what. I'll be here tomorrow after work. You can decide then what you want to do."

"Thanks. When this is all over with, I owe you a dinner. No, a banquet."

"I'll take you up on that. I never turn down good food, and Gabe will take a big steak bone." Her dog nudged her hand as if he knew she was talking about food. "We're leaving, boy," then she said to Dominic, "I feed him in the evening. The word *s-t-e-a-k* is in his vocabulary."

Dominic chuckled. "I've heard of spelling around young kids, but not dogs."

"He's very smart. See he's getting restless. He wants his *f-o-o-d* now."

"Go. I'll see you and him tomorrow."

As Abbey walked away with Gabe tugging on his leash, the drill of Dominic's gaze penetrated the shell she'd placed around herself since Peter had washed his hands of being a husband and father. She could help someone in need and keep it casual. Couldn't she?

"When are they going to be here?" Madi asked the next evening while she sat in her wheelchair, eagerly anticipating petting Gabe.

"Any minute. She texted me she was on the way. I think a certain young lady is getting tired of seeing just me and the staff." Dominic put his laptop in its case and set it next to the couch.

"I love seeing you. But I'm tired of being in the hospital. Again."

"I know. Hopefully this will be the last time. The doctor thinks this operation will be successful." In the six months since the crash, she'd spent over four of them in the hospital or a rehab center. She'd missed the second semester of third grade and was trying to catch up when she felt well enough to do her schoolwork. He would soon have to get a tutor for her, so in the fall she could go on to the fourth grade with her classmates.

"I hate physical therapy." She looked down at the wheelchair and slapped her hand against the padded arm. "I hate this thing."

Like so many times before, his sister went through a range of emotions within a short period of time. He knelt in front of her. "It won't be long before you'll be walking again."

When she lifted her head, tears glistened in her eyes. "I miss..." She opened her mouth then snapped it closed.

"What do you miss, hon?"

"Nothing." She slumped over and stared at her lap. "I'm okay."

He wanted to say, *No, you aren't. Tell me what's wrong. I'll fix it.* But then he wondered if he really could take care of her problems. He wasn't her father—only her brother—half brother at that. Before all this had happened, he'd only seen her a few times a year. "I'll be here for you, especially if things aren't okay. You know that, don't you?" he finally asked.

Her gaze sought his, and she nodded, then flung her arms around his neck. "I love you."

"And I love you."

The sound of a knock at the door chased away Madi's tears as she straightened and peered at the entrance. "Come in," she shouted for half the floor to hear.

Dominic rose, looking forward to seeing Abbey and her dog again. Two days ago he would have been surprised at the change, but if it would help his sister get better, he would try anything. And from what he saw on Madi's face—a big, beaming smile—this was just what she needed.

The door swung open, and Abbey and Gabe entered the room. She unleashed the dog, and he trotted over to Madi as though no one else was around. This time she threw her arms around Gabe and buried her face against his body.

"I've got a ball for you. The nurse told me how much

Gabe loves playing catch." Madi produced a rubber one she'd asked Dominic to buy for her. She held it up and shook her hand back and forth then slammed the ball against the floor. It bounced several times while Gabe went after it and caught it in midair, then padded to Dominic's sister and dropped it in her lap.

As she threw it again, Dominic backed away by the door with Abbey next to him. "I wonder when the nurse will come in and shut this down."

"Caron's on duty. It'll be a while. Besides, there's no one on the other side of the room."

"So we only have to worry about the offices below us?"

"I have a feeling Madison will get tired before that." She tossed her head in the direction of his sister, who was letting the ball almost roll off her hand now.

"She's been sleeping a lot today but insisted on being up and in her wheelchair when you and Gabe came. The nurse's aide even combed and fixed her hair. She didn't like my attempt at a ponytail. According to her, I haven't got the technique down like it should be."

The sound of the ball striking the floor stopped. Dominic glanced toward Madi. His sister had Gabe perched on the arm of her chair so she could be eye to eye with the dog. Low murmurs came from her, and he noticed she was whispering into Gabe's ear.

"Do you mind if Abbey and I go get some coffee from the machine down the hall? We'll leave Gabe. Okay?"

"Go ahead. Gabe will keep me company. Won't you, boy?"

Abbey's dog barked.

Out in the hall, before Dominic took two steps, his

cell phone rang. He dug into his pocket and answered a call he'd been expecting. He held up a finger to indicate just a moment to Abbey, then turned his back and said, "I hope you have good news, Samuel."

"Our employees were returned to us, but…"

Dominic's stomach dropped.

Chapter Four

"But?" Abbey heard Dominic ask in a voice full of dread.

Whatever it was, it wasn't good. Although his back was to Abbey, his body stiffened and the grip he had on his cell phone tightened until she glimpsed white knuckles.

"Okay. Let me know what arrangements you make." When he disconnected the call, he remained facing down the hall for a long moment before he swung around. For a few seconds, pain had a hold of his face until he masked it behind a neutral expression.

"What's wrong?" She prayed it was nothing concerning Madison.

"My three employees who were held for ransom were released, but one is dead. Apparently, from what Samuel said, he died of a heart attack two days ago. They neglected to say that until after they got their ransom money. Samuel is arranging for the two employees and the body of the third man to be flown back to Houston as soon as possible, but it may take some time. They're at the U.S. embassy right now."

Abbey bridged the distance between them. "I'm so sorry. Does he have a family?"

"Robert has a wife and two teenage sons." He clamped his jaw so tight a muscle twitched in his cheek. "This settles it. I'm shutting down the factory in Costa Sierra. If other people think they can get away with doing this, I'll have more employees kidnapped. I won't put my people in danger like that."

She wished she could erase the anguish she saw in his face but knew he had to work through this new grief. There wasn't a shortcut to grieving. Trying to forget certainly didn't work. She'd tried that. "It sounds like you've been thinking about closing the factory for a while."

"Ever since the rebels started causing trouble, but the government assured me my people were safe in the capital. Obviously they aren't. I can't have my company become a pawn in a game between two warring factions in the country. I'll find other ways to help the local people who work in my factory down there."

"How many Costa Sierrans work for you at the factory?"

"A hundred and ten. I'm afraid they'll be targeted next since they work for an American company." Dominic massaged his fingertips into his temples. "I need a gallon of coffee. I have a feeling I'll be up tonight trying to make sure my employees are safely back in Houston as soon as possible, as well as talking to Robert's widow. I'll have to wait until Madi's asleep before I make any calls. I don't want her to know. It'll just upset her. She has such a soft heart."

"Why don't you go make your calls and get some coffee? Gabe and I will sit with her." She could tell he was about to decline, so she added, "She's smart. She'll be able to tell something's wrong. Remember, I said I could give you a break, if you needed one."

He plowed his fingers through his hair. "I used to be quite good at hiding my feelings from others. I'm slipping."

"No, you're just tired. You've been sleeping on a cot in Madison's hospital room. Go. I'll let her know you'll be back shortly. Do what you need to do." She waved her hands as if shooing him away.

Dominic smiled. "Yes, ma'am. I'll be in the waiting room down the hall. There shouldn't be too many people in there at this time of day." He took out a business card and wrote something on the back. "If you need me, call me on my cell phone. I can be back in the room in less than a minute."

"Quit worrying. I'll be able to handle Madi. If Gabe is doing his job, she won't even notice you're gone. Well, maybe a little, but nothing to worry about."

He started toward the vending machines at the end of the hall, paused near her and clasped her upper arm. "Thanks. I'll feel more settled if I know everything has been taken care of properly."

"But didn't you say you had a good person in charge right now in Houston? If that's the case, let him do his job. You can't do everything yourself all the time. I learned that the hard way." *When my husband left.* But she couldn't share that with him.

"I have little choice. I can't be there while Madi is here. But when it's important, it's hard to let the control go."

"I know. You're talking to the former world's most organized person."

"Former?"

"When my life fell apart, so did the organization and schedule I thought I needed to function efficiently as a wife, mother and student. It didn't matter in the long run. What I ended up learning is that I'm really not in control. God is."

When his hand fell away from her, she missed his touch. In three years she hadn't allowed herself to get close to anyone. As he headed toward the coffee machine, she opened the door to Madison's room. The child's wheelchair wasn't visible from the entrance so she didn't know Abbey had returned.

"Gabe, thanks for listening. Abbey was right. You're a good listener, and I don't have to worry about you telling anyone what happened in the plane."

Abbey backed out and reentered the room, making a lot of noise as she did. When she came into Madison's view, Abbey smiled. "I hope Gabe has entertained you with all his tricks."

"We were just getting to that. What does he know?"

"The usual, but there are a few I'll have to show you later. I don't have the right equipment for him to do them here."

"What are they?"

"A surprise. Something you can look forward to when you leave the hospital."

"But that won't be for days." Madison pouted.

"Think of it like Christmas. The anticipation is half the fun."

"Nope. I think unwrapping the presents is *all* the fun."

Abbey sat on the couch and leaned toward Madison. "I'll tell you a secret. Gabe feels the same way. I have to hide his Christmas gift, or he'd have it unwrapped the second I turn my back. In fact, all my dogs and cats are like that. I think they learned it from him."

Madison rubbed his fur. "I knew it. You and I are a lot alike, Gabe." The child scanned the room. "Where's Dominic?"

"He'll be right back. He has a couple of business calls to make, and I didn't want him disrupting our visit with them. Okay?"

"Yeah, he sure likes to talk on his cell phone. I can't image having that much to say to another person."

Abbey pressed her lips together to keep from laughing. In a few years that would all change. "You don't talk to your friends on the phone?"

"I used to but not much lately. I haven't felt like it. All they wanted to talk about is what they're doing at school, and now that it's summer, they're all playing and having fun." Hurt mixed with jealousy laced Madison's voice.

"You can play and have fun. You're getting much better, and before you know it, you'll be as good as new."

"I guess." A frown flirted with the corners of Madison's mouth.

"Have they come to visit you?"

"A little but I can't do much with them. They used to come over, and we'd go riding. But I haven't ridden a horse since—" Madi swallowed hard "—since my accident."

"Then that can be something you work toward. I have a friend who owns a stable where she does horse therapy with kids who have physical issues."

"Really?"

"It's something your brother can look into if your doctor and physical therapist agree."

"What can I look into?" Dominic asked as he stepped into the room.

"Madison misses riding. I was telling her about a friend of mine who helps people with physical problems ride a horse."

Madison twisted around to see him behind her. "Dominic, please, please find out if I can."

The look he shot Abbey told her she'd overstepped again, but when he came into Madi's view, his expression didn't reveal his displeasure. "I will, but as Abbey pointed out, I need to see what the doctor says first. Your incisions haven't healed yet."

Before he changed his mind about letting Gabe visit Abbey, she said, "I'd better be going. I still have to pick up the new dog at Dad's."

"You're getting another dog?" Madison asked.

"Only temporarily, until I find a good home for her."

"Her? What kind is she?" The child continued to stroke Gabe.

"A bichon frise. She's small and white with a curly tail."

"Like a pig?"

"Sorta." Abbey put the leash on her Lab. "We'll see you tomorrow. I'll be here after work."

"I'll walk you to the elevator." Dominic followed her toward the door. "Be back in a minute, Madi."

Before he could say anything to her in the hall, Abbey asked, "Did you get everything settled about your employees?"

"Yes, but that's not what I want to talk to you about."

She grinned. "I know. I shouldn't have said anything

to Madison without asking you first." She lifted her arms in a shrug. "What can I say? I'm a work in progress." She pushed the button for the elevator. "Those bulldog characteristics won't disappear overnight."

"You aren't in the least bit contrite over what you did."

"Yes, I am. But I will say Madison working with Tory would be good for your sister since she loves to ride horses. Or maybe her physical therapist is familiar enough to show you what to do with Madison."

As the elevator arrived and she got on it, Dominic shook his head, but a laugh escaped his mouth. She waved at him as the doors slid shut. Gabe looked up at her. "We've got our work cut out for us, boy. Those two are definitely in need of our services. We're both good listeners, and they have a lot bottled up inside them." Although she was pretty sure Madison had confided in Gabe while she and Dominic had been in the hallway, the little girl needed to talk to someone about her feelings concerning the plane crash.

As the elevator opened on the ground floor, Abbey couldn't stop wondering what had Madison troubled.

Dominic's housekeeper opened the door to Abbey, looked her up and down, then fixed her gaze on Gabe before returning her attention to Abbey. She pursed her lips and said, "Mr. Winters called and told me a young lady was coming with a dog to be here when Madison comes home. I'm assuming you're that person."

"Yes. I wanted to surprise her."

"Madison doesn't like surprises."

Abbey held out her hand. "I'm Abbey Harris."

The housekeeper stepped back and said, "Please

come in. You can wait in the foyer with your dog." Then the woman, who was around fifty, with a touch of gray at the temples, headed toward the hallway. "I must finish the cake I made for Madison's homecoming."

Abbey dropped her arm to her side and watched the housekeeper disappear. "Well, Gabe, it's just you and me."

She glanced around the large foyer, which was bigger than her bedroom, then peeked into the living and dining rooms opposite each other. The entry with its marble floor, a large mahogany round table in the middle with fresh-cut flowers in a crystal vase and an antique sideboard with pieces of Western sculpture set the tone for the house—wealthy elegance.

Abbey prowled the foyer with Gabe on his leash next to her, pausing in the entrance to the living room. The first impression was that it wasn't kid-friendly. Splashes of gold and blue broke the sea of white, but even the carpet was white. No wonder the housekeeper wasn't too pleased to have Gabe in the house. There wasn't a speck of dirt or dust visible anywhere.

At the sound of the door opening, Abbey turned and saw Dominic and Madison entering the house. He pushed the wheelchair with his sister sitting in it, her legs in soft casts. His gaze immediately found Abbey's. Though weary lines were engraved on his face, Dominic grinned at her.

Abbey turned her attention to the girl. A cheerless demeanor enveloped the child, sagging her shoulders, and her stare was fastened squarely on her lap. Abbey unhooked Gabe from his leash, and he padded across the foyer. The click of his toenails against the marble floor caused Madison to look up. She immediately beamed and reached out toward the dog. Her arms surrounded Gabe, and she laid her head against him.

Dominic came to stand in front of his sister. "See? Didn't I tell you that you would see Gabe soon?"

Madison lifted her head. "Did you know they were gonna be here?"

"Maybe."

His sister clamped her lips in a tight, thin line for a few seconds, then burst into giggles. "That's mean. I kept asking you where Gabe and Abbey were, and you wouldn't tell me."

"You might not like surprises, but I love surprising a certain little girl. I asked him not to say anything."

Madison peered at Abbey as she closed the gap between them. "I thought you forgot I was leaving the hospital today."

"Never, but I don't like saying goodbye. Much better to welcome someone home. I hope you're glad you're home now." Abbey stopped next to Gabe, who was sitting patiently while Madison gave him the attention he loved.

"Yes. Yes! Finally. I thought this last time would be *forever*."

"I can imagine how sick you are of spending time in the hospital, but each time you're getting better and better." Abbey had gone through this with her daughter, which helped her anticipate how the child felt.

Madison gestured toward her casts. "I don't call this better. I'm still in a wheelchair."

"Only until the doctor says you can start working with your P.T. to walk again." Dominic pushed the wheelchair. "I've got another surprise for you in the den."

"You do?" Madison glanced over her shoulder.

"Come this way, ladies."

"And Gabe?" Abbey asked, looking at all the white carpet.

"Definitely. He needs to give his seal of approval." Dominic paused and waited for Abbey and her dog to follow.

When Abbey came into the den with Gabe, she stopped, amazed at the difference in this room compared to the others she'd glimpsed since entering the house. It was as large as the living room, but with a feel of cozy comfort. The leather couches and chairs invited a person to relax, even put his feet up on the cushions. The furniture was arranged around a large hearth with a big TV screen over the mantel. Bookcases lined one wall while another was a bank of floor-to-ceiling windows that afforded a view of a well-landscaped backyard with a pool and cabana.

But what drew Abbey and Madison's attention was the electric wheelchair in the center of the room near a massive oak coffee table.

"How fast does it go?" Madison leaned over to touch the controls on the right arm.

"Hold it right there, kiddo. No way will you race around this house. Slow is the only speed you're going to use."

Madison's mouth went from a smile to a pout instantly. "Aw, you know how to take the fun out of something new."

"Besides, in the house your physical therapist wants you to use your manual wheelchair. This one is for when you want to go outside. Maybe down to the barn." Dominic said, squatting and putting one arm under her legs and the other around her back, then transferring her to the new electric wheelchair. "I have another surprise for you."

Madison locked her hands together around his neck. "What?"

"Miss Impatience, give me a chance to show you how to use—"

Madison put the wheelchair into a forward motion and made a large circular path in the den around the grouping of couches and chairs with only one mishap when she drove into the long table behind one of the sofas. A vase wobbled near Abbey, and she lunged toward it, catching it before it toppled to the floor.

"I think I need to adjust the speed. You're going a little too fast."

"You call this fast?" Madison headed toward the exit.

Dominic hurriedly planted himself in front of the doorway. Madison came to a quick halt, then put the wheelchair in Reverse. Gabe scrambled out of the way. Dominic leaped toward the chair and switched it off in back.

"What's the problem? I don't need to learn how to operate it. It's easy. Push this to go forward and pull it to go backward. Piece of cake." Madison giggled. "You did have Mrs. Ponder make my favorite cake, didn't you? Is that the surprise?"

"Maybe, maybe not." Dominic hovered over the right arm of the wheelchair in case his sister decided to put it in motion again. "Aren't you ready for a nap? I sure am."

Madison's laughter increased. "No, I'm tired of being in bed and sleeping."

"It's only been six days since your surgery."

"Forever when you're stuck in a hospital room."

"You weren't in your room all the time."

Abbey decided to step in. "What's the other surprise? Madison may have forgotten about it, but I haven't and I am definitely impatient."

"Yeah, what is it?" Madison directed her look at her brother.

"If you hadn't interrupted me with your antics, I'd have shown it to you by now."

"I'm not stopping you now."

He shook his head and started for the hallway. "Mrs. Ponder told me I would regret getting you an electric wheelchair for places that would be hard to roll your other one."

With Abbey next to the girl, Madison trailed after her brother. Gabe hung back and didn't come when Abbey patted her hand against her leg. Abbey stopped and looked back a few seconds at her dog.

The child frowned. "What's wrong? Gabe, come on. I want you to see my surprise, too."

Gabe's tail swept the floor, but he stayed put.

That was when Abbey remembered an incident with another kid at the hospital the week before. "I think he's scared of your electric wheelchair. A little boy ran over his tail with one. Gabe yelped and refused to visit the child again."

"I don't blame him, but I wouldn't do that, boy." Madison slapped her hand on the top of her thigh. "Come, Gabe. Please."

Her dog barked twice.

"That's his no."

"What's his yes?" Dominic asked from the entrance.

"One bark."

"Why isn't he scared of my other wheelchair?" Madison turned her chair completely around and moved toward the Lab.

Gabe stood and backed away, positioning himself between the coffee table and couch where Madison couldn't go.

"Gabe knows the difference. I haven't had a chance to work with him yet on getting used to the electric one."

Madison glanced at her brother. "Will you move me to the other wheelchair for now? I don't want him to be afraid of me."

"Are you sure?"

With her solemn gaze fixed on Gabe, Madison nodded.

Dominic transferred his sister back to the manual chair. "Let's go. I'll even run with you."

Before Madison could say anything, he pushed her out into the hall at twice the speed he had coming into the house. Abbey signaled to Gabe to come to her side. Her Lab made a wide detour around the abandoned electric wheelchair. Abbey hooked the leash to his collar and headed into the hallway to find that Dominic had parked Madison in front of a panel wall.

Madison grinned from ear to ear. "My very own elevator?"

"Yep. I can use the stairs. It'll keep me in shape. I've got to do something now that I'm not pushing you around. I can't lose my manly figure."

Madison's laughter sprinkled the air.

And brought a smile to Abbey. When she neared the pair halfway down the hall, she saw Madison's surprise—an elevator.

"Before you test this baby out, I want to show you

what else I've done while you were in the hospital. This way." He rolled his sister to a door at the very end of the hall and came around to open it. "This will be where you can work with your physical and occupational therapists. Everything will be handled here. You probably figured you'd have to go back to the rehab center, but not now."

Abbey moved closer and peeked inside. When she looked at Madison, tears shone in the child's eyes.

"Thank you. I don't want others see me try to walk."

Dominic clasped her shoulder and squeezed her gently. "I know. You hated going, but soon you'll be having some kind of therapy every day." He inhaled a deep breath then swung the wheelchair around and went down another hallway. "I'm not through yet with your surprises."

Abbey glimpsed the parallel bars and other pieces of equipment before hurrying after the pair as they disappeared around the corner. The aroma of a cake baking grew stronger the closer she came to Dominic and Madison.

Brother and sister entered the kitchen. The housekeeper removed three round cake pans from the oven and set them on a wire rack, then returned to a large bowl at the mixer. Mrs. Ponder nodded toward Dominic but barely acknowledged the child as he crossed the room to the back door. As Abbey followed them, the older woman threw her a cold glance, especially when it fell on Gabe at her side.

When Dominic opened the back door, a ramp stretched out from it. "We have one in front, but I wanted you to feel you could go anywhere you wanted. That's why I got you the electric wheelchair. To give you some freedom. The past months you've been confined inside. I know how much you like to visit the horses at the barn, so I've had a path laid that will enable you to do that easily in your electric wheelchair. When you use a walker or crutches later, the path will make it easier then, too."

Over Dominic's shoulder Abbey spied the black barn in the distance, with a sidewalk that led to it from the back of the house. Horses grazed in black fenced pastures nearby. Not far from the pool sat a large yellow playhouse, and it even had a ramp to allow Madison to go inside.

"I want you to do what you used to as much as possible." Dominic rolled Madison outside onto the deck—which ran the length of the back of the large house.

"Can I go to the barn? I want to see Spice."

"Sure. I thought you might so I had Chad make sure to bring Spice in from the pasture for you."

"I need to take some carrots."

"I'll get some for you." Dominic went back into the kitchen.

Gabe tugged on his leash. Abbey stepped toward Madison so Gabe could be next to her. "You have a fun backyard."

"Daddy built that playhouse for me a couple of years ago. I used to love playing in it, especially when my friends came over, but…"

Abbey came around to face Madison. "Well, now that you're home, you can see your friends again."

She shook her head. "I don't want to. Not like this. I can't do what they can. I…"

Dominic strode from the house with several carrots in his grasp. He glanced from Abbey to Madison. "What's wrong?"

"Madison was just telling me about her playhouse." Abbey intended to say something to Dominic later about reconnecting his sister with some of her friends. The child needed to be around others her age, to get some fun back into her life.

"There should be room for you to turn around in the playhouse. I checked it out." Dominic passed the carrots to Madison, who perked up when she saw them. "Let's go visit Spice. Your cake should be ready by the time we get back. We'll have Mrs. Ponder cut some slices for us. It's your favorite, chocolate with vanilla icing."

Abbey walked next to Madison. "I don't know about you, but my mouth is watering just thinking about it."

"Yeah, I guess so." Madison's shoulders slumped, and she stared at the carrots in her lap.

"When was the last time you saw Spice?" Abbey asked, watching the child's body language.

"The day before the accident." Madison shifted around and peered at Abbey. "What if she forgot who I am? It's been a long time."

"She won't have forgotten you. Lots of animals have a long memory when it comes to stuff like that."

"I hope so."

Dominic arrived at the yard in front of the barn. "Look who is coming out to greet you."

The girl lifted her head. "Spice!"

Walking bowlegged, a cowboy, probably in his fifties, led a pinto out of the open double doors toward Madison. "My lands, child, she saw you coming and began prancing around. Here, would you like to hold her reins?"

"Do you think she missed me, Uncle Chad?"

"She's been pining for you. I usually keep her in this paddock next to the barn, and she hangs out at this here fence, watching the back door at the house."

Spice dropped her head near Madison while the girl held up a carrot for the pinto to munch. When there were no more carrots, the horse nudged the child until she began stroking Spice's nose.

"I'm thinking she remembers you and misses you." Uncle Chad winked at Madison. "If there's one thing I know, it's horses."

Gabe planted himself next to the wheelchair and watched the exchange between Spice and Madison. The pinto finally acknowledged the dog's existence by sniffing him. Gabe let her. When Spice returned to Madison, Gabe yelped once.

"Gabe approves of Spice." Abbey moved closer to Dominic while giving Gabe more of the leash.

Madison's expression emphasized how important animals were to her. She connected to Spice, but she also took time to rub Gabe and give him attention while all three acquainted themselves with the others. Abbey immediately thought of the abandoned dog she'd taken in. She hadn't named her yet, and she was beginning to think that was because she thought the bichon would be perfect for Madison.

"I'd like to bring the little dog I just took in to meet your sister. I think Madison and the bichon would get along great," Abbey whispered to Dominic, not wanting the child to hear in case her brother didn't agree.

"Do you really think it's a good idea to try to replace Zoe so soon? They went everywhere together. Zoe even slept with Madi."

"I think it's worth seeing if it would work."

"We'll see. So much with Madi is up in the air until she heals."

"But a lot of it doesn't have to be. A kid needs to feel everything around her is the same where it can be. Routine gives comfort. The familiar does, too." Abbey had worked hard to make sure Lisa's life was as normal as possible even in the middle of the fight for her life.

"We'll let Madi decide what she wants after she spends some time with the dog. I think Gabe will be hard to replace." Dominic grinned. "He's a charmer and reminds me of my golden retriever the more I'm around him."

"Yeah, he senses what others need and tries to give it to them."

"Unless they're in an electric wheelchair."

"He does have his limits, unfortunately."

Dominic's gaze snagged hers. "How about you?"

"Everyone does," Abbey said with a chuckle. But behind his expression was a seriousness, as though he'd been questioning his own limits. She remembered doing that about this time after her daughter died.

"The end," Abbey said, and closed the book she'd read to Madison in her bedroom later that evening.

Madison's eyebrows scrunched together. "But it's not the end. I want to know if Nancy Drew catches the thief."

"It's the end of chapter six. Dominic will have to read you the next one tomorrow night."

"Why can't you?"

"Because I won't be here."

"You read so much better than my brother. You use different voices for the different people."

"My dad used to do that when he read me stories."

Madison's eyes clouded. "My dad never read a story to me. It was always my mom. I miss them."

"Of course you do." Abbey hoped the child would say more about her parents.

Gabe lay on top of the covers near Madison with his head resting in her lap. She stroked him over and over. "Don't tell Dominic he doesn't read as good as you. I don't want him to stop reading to me."

Abbey acted as if she were zipping her lips. "He won't hear it from me."

"He's trying his best."

Abbey placed the Nancy Drew book on the nightstand, her hand quivering. She'd loved the series as a child. Now she would never get the chance to read a Nancy Drew book to Lisa. "What do you mean?" Abbey curled her hands into fists to still the slight trembling.

Madison leaned toward Abbey and lowered her voice. "He doesn't know what to do with me. He's never had a little girl. All he's ever done is work. At least that's what my parents used to say. 'Dominic can't come. He's overseas.'" She tilted her head as she sank back against the pillows. "What does that mean?"

"It means he's out of the country. I imagine his work involves a lot of traveling."

Gabe lifted his head and looked toward the door. "Shh. That's probably him coming," Madison said.

Dominic came into the room not ten seconds later. "Sorry about that delay. I had to take the call. Are you ready for me to read the next chapter, kiddo?"

"Abbey already did. She read Nancy Drew when she was my age."

"Yep, I went on a journey down memory lane." Abbey rose to allow Dominic closer to his sister. When he'd first appeared in the doorway, she'd seen a struggle taking place within Dominic—as though he were fighting to keep an upbeat expression on his face. Something was wrong.

"She knows what happens in the story and won't tell me."

"There would be no reason to read the rest of the book if she did."

"Oh, I guess you're right. Can Gabe spend the night?"

Her dog's ears perked forward at the mention of his name. He barked once.

"He said yes. So can he?" Madison turned her big eyes on her brother.

Abbey decided to rescue Dominic by saying, "He can't. Corky and Ginger, my other two dogs, will be waiting for him to come home."

"How about your new dog? Are they friends yet?" Madison absently petted Gabe as she talked.

"They're getting to know each other. She hasn't been there long."

"What's her name?"

"I haven't come up with one yet."

"She's gotta have a name. How will she know when you're calling her?"

"Good point. Do you two want to help me name her?" Abbey glanced from Madison to Dominic, who appeared more relaxed than when he'd first come into the room.

Madison covered a yawn. "I'd have to meet her first. Just another reason you should bring her here to visit." Another yawn escaped from the child.

"It's way past your bedtime, young lady." Dominic bent down and kissed her forehead then helped tuck his sister into bed.

"But we haven't come up with a time…" Madison's eyes drooped closed for a few seconds before snapping open. "A time for Abbey to bring over the new dog."

"I'll talk with Abbey and let you know tomorrow. Good night, kiddo."

Abbey signaled to Gabe to hop down, but not before Madison rubbed her face against his neck. "I hope you'll come visit again. I'll only use my old wheelchair when you're here. Okay, boy?" The child stroked his ears then kissed him before snuggling down under her covers.

Abbey walked with Gabe toward the hallway while Dominic turned on the night-light and switched off the bedside lamp. He left the door open when he came out of the room. In silence Abbey and Dominic made their way downstairs, but the second he wasn't with his sister, Dominic's upbeat expression collapsed.

In the foyer, Abbey rotated toward him. "The new dog is up to you."

"I'm fine with that. We can work out something around your schedule and Madi's physical therapy, which starts tomorrow. I'm glad she's back home and in her own room. I think that will help her."

"I agree, but that isn't what's bothering you, is it? What's wrong?"

Tension tightened his features. His eyes darkened.

Something was wrong, but he didn't trust her enough to tell her. Abbey ducked her head, disappointment spreading through her.

Chapter Five

Dominic faced Abbey in the foyer, his breath trapped in his lungs until they burned. He released a swoosh of air and massaged the back of his neck, the tension down his spine making it feel as if a steel rod held him upright. "Have you ever been torn in two different directions?"

"Sure. When I was a mother and wife trying to also finish my master's degree, I often felt like three different people and had a hard time juggling those roles. Is this about your work and your sister?"

"Am I that obvious?" He tried to smile, but it didn't stay long.

"I know you received a call from Samuel, and when you came back to say good-night to Madison, you were struggling to stay cheerful. I could see something was bothering you, and you were trying not to let Madison see."

"Do you think she knows something is wrong?"

"She's sharp, but she was tired and too busy trying to get you to read another chapter of Nancy Drew." Abbey looked around then moved back to the stairs and sat. "It's been a long day. What's happening?"

He joined her, feeling the past months crashing down on him. Gabe sat on the floor between them, and Dominic reached out to stroke the dog. "I need to go to the funeral Friday. My employee's body was delayed returning from Costa Sierra, and now the family can finally bury him. I want to be there for them. They have gone through so much. I also need to talk with my other two employees in person. I thought of flying them here, but they need to be with their families in familiar surroundings. They went through a horrible ordeal because they're my employees." An invisible band about his chest tightened.

"And you have Madison here needing your support, as well? Is that what you're thinking?"

He nodded, not sure he could formulate the necessary words to explain his dilemma adequately. "Madi wakes up every night from bad dreams. I've tried to get her to tell me about them, but all she wants to do is cling to me. I have a monitor in her room, but even with it, I don't know she's having a nightmare until she's crying out. Her covers are all twisted up, so the dream has to be going on for a while."

"Gabe is good at detecting when a nightmare is starting. I've dealt with this before with my daughter. I know how hard it can be. I know…" Abbey's words faded, and she averted her gaze.

Pain flitted through her expression. She swallowed hard and chewed on her lower lip, her stare fastened on the floor.

"I'm sorry, Abbey. This is stirring up memories that are hard for you."

A long silence hovered between them before she asked, "How long do you need to be in Houston?"

"I could leave late Thursday afternoon and be back Saturday night. I want to attend the wake Thursday evening and the funeral Friday, then meet with my other employees on Saturday. Do you think Madi would be all right with Mrs. Ponder? She lives here and could watch Madi."

Abbey frowned. "If you're asking me, then you already have reservations about leaving your sister alone with your housekeeper."

"Yes. She tolerates Madi, but she sees it as her duty to keep the house clean and cook the meals, not babysit. She's very good at that job, but she isn't a nanny. She came to work for my father fifteen years ago when he didn't have a child."

"But she isn't what you need right now?"

"I need someone to keep this place in order, and I'm certainly not a cook. I can throw some simple dishes together if I had to. But I need more now with Madi." The feel of Gabe's fur beneath his palm reminded Dominic of his dog, Rocket. He and his golden retriever had gone everywhere on the ranch, getting into one adventure after another. He could see why Madi responded to Gabe.

"Have you thought of hiring someone to help with Madison?"

"Yes, but this isn't the time to bring a stranger into her life. I can't do that and leave for Houston on Friday. I've even thought of taking Madi with me, but I still would have to leave her at my apartment in Houston with someone."

"Madison needs familiarity."

"I know, especially now that she is back at the ranch with no more visits to the hospital."

Abbey nibbled her lip for a moment, then spoke. "I think I've got a solution for you, Dominic. Me."

He looked at her, glimpsing a shadow that dulled her eyes as if she wasn't completely convinced by her words. "I can't ask you to do that."

"I won't kid you that being with Madison hasn't stirred memories of my daughter and the heartache I went through. It has, but the bottom line is Madison's well-being. In a short time, I've come to care about your sister and want to see her get better. Her mental health is important to that process. You should be in Houston for the funeral, and Madison should have someone familiar with her who can devote time to her while you're gone."

"But you have a job at the hospital."

"I have flexible hours and can do some of my work from here. Madison and I have gotten to know each other this past week, and you've seen how taken she is with Gabe. When she's feeling lonely, he can be here to chase the sadness away."

He shook his head. "I hate to ask you to do that."

"You're not. I'm offering. It would be a great time to get Gabe used to an electric wheelchair. I can't have my therapy dog running scared when he sees one. I also can bring the bichon frise over for Madison to see."

"Mrs. Ponder probably wouldn't be too happy about that."

"Ah, you've seen the glares she's sent Gabe."

"Kind of hard to miss," he said with a smile, feeling the steel rod down his spine start to soften. "When we were eating dinner, and he was lying by Madi's chair,

I'm sure Mrs. Ponder was just waiting for Gabe to jump up and take the fried chicken off Madi's plate."

"Yeah, she was hovering. But I can deal with Mrs. Ponder."

Dominic wasn't so sure that was true, but he was willing to give it a try. He nodded to Abbey in agreement.

"Then it's settled. I'll stay with Madison Thursday when you leave until you return."

"Only if you'll accept some kind of payment for your services."

She shot him a narrow-eyed look. "No. I'm doing this for Madison. Pay makes it a job. This isn't a job to me. I want to do this because I care about Madison."

He stood. "But I don't want to impose—"

Her hand covered his mouth. "Stop. Not another word about it, or I will retract my offer." She flashed him a smile. "Besides, I can't go around avoiding girls who would be my daughter's age if she were alive, especially in my job at the hospital."

The feel of her fingers on his mouth sent a wave of awareness through him. This woman was caring, giving and beautiful. A deadly combination when he was trying to avoid all kinds of romantic entanglements. When she dropped her arm to her side, he missed her touch. When he went out with women in Houston, it had always been casual, usually for business functions. He'd made it clear he had no time for a permanent relationship. His feelings hadn't changed, and Abbey deserved more than that.

"Then at least let me take you to a dinner as a thank-you sometime."

"It's a deal. I now have two dinners you owe me. I'll

even let you take me to the most expensive restaurant in town. Will that make you feel better?"

Dominic grinned. "Most definitely."

"Good. Now I'd better go. As I said earlier, it's been a long day." Abbey crossed the foyer.

He followed, and leaned in to open the front door. "I'll call you about the time I'll need to leave on Thursday."

"If you have to go earlier, let me know. I'm going to get everything done tomorrow so I can be available earlier on Thursday if that works out better."

He took her hand in his and held it up between them, his gaze trained on her. "Thank you. I appreciate this. I had no intention of asking you to look after Madi, but when you brought it up, I knew it was the perfect solution to my dilemma." Especially after he'd asked various people at the hospital about Abbey. Madi's doctors and the rest of the staff had only glowing things to say about Abbey. A few had mentioned how much Gabe had helped other patients while they were at the hospital.

The smile that lit her brown eyes pulled him toward her. It took all his efforts not to bridge the space between them and kiss her. He wasn't ready to share his life with someone, not with Madi's health still tenuous, but there was something about Abbey that drew him unlike any other woman.

"If something comes up and you need me to stay until Sunday, I can extend my time here. I'll have Dad come over and take care of my pets so that won't be a problem."

"Let's see how Madi reacts. If things are going all right, I could then meet with my department heads on

Saturday and the employees and their families on Sunday."

"Good. You should utilize the time in Houston while you have it. See you and Madison tomorrow after work."

"Are you sure?"

"I promised her I would come see her and bring Gabe before we made these arrangements. It's important I keep that promise. She's learning to trust me. Okay?"

A grin from deep inside him completely vanquished the tension gripping him. Looking into her expression relaxed him. "It's fine with me. Should I tell Mrs. Ponder you'll stay for dinner again tomorrow night?"

"No. I'll need to give the pets I leave at home some extra attention while I pack. See you." She swung around and led Gabe toward her car, parked on the side where he'd told her to hide it from Madi.

Dominic watched her drive away from his house. *His home now.* He still wasn't used to thinking like that. His father had left the ranch to him and everything on it, while he'd left a large trust for Madi. One way or another his father had been determined Dominic would run Winter Haven Ranch. His father had never cared that Dominic had created his own company with thousands of people working for him. He'd wanted Dominic to run the family ranch ever since he could remember.

He scanned the dark landscape from the front deck, imagining the horses his father had raised for the rodeo circuit while also having a large herd of cattle. This wasn't his life anymore. But it would always be his home, and Madi's.

A woman at the nursing home saw Abbey coming into the building and stepped into her path. She'd seen

her once visiting the lady across from Mr. Johnson.
Abbey smiled at her, intending to hurry toward Mr.
Johnson's room. She was late because of last-minute
preparations for staying with Madison this weekend.

"Are you the one who brings a dog for some of the
patients here?" the middle-aged woman asked Abbey.

"Yes." Abbey paused with Gabe right next to her
on a leash while she held the bichon frise in her arms.

"I want to thank you for letting my mother join you
and Mr. Johnson out in the courtyard. That's all she's
been talking about the past few days. It's brightened
her day. I worry, though, when the weather gets too
hot, about her being outside."

"I'll be glad to do it in the recreation room, but you
need to talk with Mrs. Rosen. She's the one who said if
I bring Gabe, we have to be outside. She doesn't even
want me coming inside with him, but this is the only
way to the enclosed courtyard." Abbey saw Mrs. Rosen
heading toward her. "I need to go. I'm sure Mr. Johnson
and the others are wondering where I am."

"But—"

"Sorry, can't keep them waiting."

Abbey quickened her pace down the hallway to the
door that led out into the courtyard. For the past week
she'd come over to see Mr. Johnson several times after
seeing Madison at her house. She hadn't come yesterday
or the day before so it was important to be here today.
From the gruff sound of his voice on the phone earlier,
Mr. Johnson wasn't too happy with her.

As she opened the outside door, she glanced down
the hall and found Mrs. Rosen staring at her with her
hand on her waist while the woman who had just approached her was saying something to her. The frown

that appeared on the director's face shouted her displeasure at what she was hearing.

Out in the courtyard, the sunshine bathed the tiled surface, the air warm at this time of day. At least the interior area was sheltered a lot from the wind blowing at twenty-five miles per hour. In the middle there was a gazebo where the patients were sitting, most of them in wheelchairs. June was usually nice weather, but she still had to convince Mrs. Rosen to allow Gabe or any therapy dog inside with the patients. July and August in Oklahoma had beastly temperatures, even early in the morning.

"Hi, everyone. Sorry I was running a little late, but I brought an extra treat for you all. I have this sweet little bichon that I'm taking over to a friend's house today. I thought you all might like to meet her." Abbey's gaze swept around the crowd—seven patients and a nurse's aide. There were three more patients since last time and now a nurse's aide. Was she here to find a reason to stop Abbey from coming to the home? She stepped up to the woman. "I'm Abbey Harris."

"I'm Laurie. With so many patients wanting to come, my supervisor thought I should be out here in case someone needs help." She bent close to Abbey and lowered her voice, saying, "Personally, I love this idea. I know these two ladies I take care of were excited about your visit."

"That's wonderful." Abbey turned back to the two men and five women in a semicircle. "I'll start with Gabe at this end and my new dog at the other." She unleashed Gabe because he knew the routine. He immediately went to Mr. Johnson first, while Abbey made her way to a frail lady in a wheelchair, her shoulders bent over.

"What's her name?" the delicate woman asked.

"I don't have one yet since I hope to give her to a little girl. I want her to name her."

"Yeah, you don't want to confuse the poor dog." The lady lifted her face up, her bright gaze honing in on Abbey. "My body is giving out, but my mind is sharp, and I would love to have a dog here. I used to have a poodle, white like this sweetie." She picked up the bichon and snuggled her against her cheek. "I miss this."

Abbey heard similar remarks as she passed the little dog from one patient to the next. When she reached Mr. Johnson, a scowl grooved his face.

"I didn't get enough time with Gabe. I wish you could come more. I wish I could keep him."

Abbey pulled up a chair and sat next to Mr. Johnson, then whistled for Gabe to return to her. Her Lab settled by the old man, his head in his lap. "I won't be able to come until Monday, most likely. I'm taking care of a little girl while her guardian is out of town."

"Bring her."

"She's recovering from surgery and she's in a wheelchair right now."

"Why should that be a problem?" He slapped his hand against his. "So am I."

"I'll see what I can do. I'll have to clear it with her guardian." Abbey liked the idea of taking Madison somewhere, but the girl hadn't done many normal childhood activities since the accident because of the severity of her injuries. If she stayed until Sunday evening, she definitely wanted to take Madison to church with her—if Dominic agreed. She didn't know how he felt about Jesus.

"What did Mrs. Rosen say when you gave her all the information about therapy dogs?" Mr. Johnson asked, his mouth set in his usual somber expression.

"Not a whole lot."

"She probably hates animals. I've known people like that. But she hasn't met someone like me. I won't sit by and not say something if I think it's wrong. I've been talking to a few of the residents—organizing the troops."

For a rebellion? She could picture Mr. Johnson leading a march of wheelchairs down the hallway. "Let me see what I can do first. I had the daughter of a resident ask me about her mother having some interaction with a pet, and I sent her to Mrs. Rosen."

Mr. Johnson snapped his fingers. "Great idea. I'll get everyone to have their families say something." He winked. "Don't you worry. I'll take care of it on this end. You find some good dogs and train them. Even ones like that froufrou dog over there." He waved his hand toward the bichon. "Some ladies will like that one. But remember, I want a manly dog."

"Yes, sir. I'll start working with my dad on that so if Mrs. Rosen says yes, we'll have some dogs ready."

"Are you *sure* I can't have Gabe?" Mr. Johnson patted the Lab continuously as he talked.

"Yes, but I'll find one you'll love as much as him, probably a little smaller. I'll still bring Gabe to see you if you want."

He snorted. "Don't think that's possible. Gabe is special. I'm warning you now. I'm gonna wear you down."

Later, as Abbey strolled from the courtyard with her

two dogs, she ran into Mrs. Rosen in the hallway. "Just because one family member thinks it would be a good idea doesn't mean it will happen, Ms. Harris. A handful of patients are taking part in your sessions. That's not many compared to the overall number of residents in the nursing home. I'm not disrupting this place for a handful."

"I understand. Perhaps, to be fair, you could let me hold a couple of 'sessions' in the rec room. Although the wind was partially blocked today in the gazebo, I still noticed that one lady was sneezing and she had to go inside earlier than she wanted. You know how bad allergies can be in Oklahoma, even in June. And I'm sure you wouldn't want the residents sitting outside in extreme heat in July and August."

"Good day, Ms. Harris." The director continued her trek toward the administration office behind the front counter in the lobby.

Not one word about the rising temperatures. Usually Abbey could keep her temper under control, but it was becoming increasingly hard with that woman. She was straight out of the Dark Ages. Abbey's blood pressure shot up. Her hands curled and uncurled as she glimpsed the director disappear into her office, the door shutting as if that would keep anything unpleasant out. But that wouldn't stop Abbey from fighting for what she thought was right.

Madi rolled her manual wheelchair into the dining room of Winter Haven Ranch, which overlooked the front driveway, and positioned herself at the window to watch for Abbey.

Dominic set his bag and briefcase on the floor in the

foyer near the door. He heard his sister come back into the foyer. "What's up, kiddo?"

"Nothing. What time is it now?"

"Five minutes later than the last time you asked."

"Shouldn't she be here by now?"

"Another five minutes. Are you sure you're okay with me going to Houston for a few days?"

Madi nodded. "Abbey is gonna bring some games for us to play. She said she had a special one if I do everything Greta tells me to do tomorrow."

"You know how important your physical therapy is, even if you can't bear weight right now."

"I like Greta. She thinks riding a horse would be good for me later."

"Once the doctor says we can, I'll look into it."

"What time is it now?" Madi asked as she made a circle and went back to the window.

"Two minutes later."

"What's taking her so long? Maybe you should call her."

Dominic leaned against the doorjamb into the dining room. Madi drummed her fingers against the arm of the wheelchair. An occasional sigh escaped her lips. He knew the second she spotted Abbey's car. His sister's expression brightened, and a huge smile replaced the worry lining her face.

"She's here!" She maneuvered around him and headed into the foyer. Each day she was becoming stronger and stronger wheeling her manual chair. Madi stopped only a foot from the door.

"I don't think they'll be able to get into the house. Move a few feet back."

After she did, she glanced over her shoulder. "Okay?"

"Perfect. You'll be the first person Gabe and Abbey see when I let them in."

As he swung the door wide, Abbey stepped up onto the deck running the length of the front of the house. Gabe trotted next to her without a leash on, and she carried a white fluffy dog. Her expression was like a ray of sunshine warming him. He hadn't realized how much he was looking forward to seeing Abbey, even if it was only for a short time before he left for Houston.

"Is that her?" Madi held out her arms for the dog. "She's like a big fat cotton ball."

"Don't let her hear you say *fat*. You know how girls are about their weight." Abbey passed the bichon to Madi.

His sister giggled. "No. They want me to eat more to gain weight."

"Oh, if I only had that problem."

Dominic's gaze skimmed down Abbey's five-foot-two-inch frame, and he thought she looked just fine.

"Will Gabe and…" Madi's mouth twisted in a thoughtful expression. "I need to come up with a good name for her." His sister lifted the dog and rubbed her cheek against her. The bichon rewarded her with several licks. "I've got it. Cottonball. How about that name?"

"I like it." Abbey saw his bag nearby. "Ready to go?"

"Yeah, we'll take my car," he said, glancing out the door at her yellow VW Beetle, "since I don't think yours will hold all of us. That way we can take the two dogs, too." He knew Madi would insist.

"Good call. I'm not sure Mrs. Ponder is ready to deal with them by herself. Cottonball is used to taking over the house, wherever she was before she came to me."

"Where's your luggage?"

"In my car. I was going to go back and get it."

"I'll do it, then we can be on our way." Dominic strode toward her car. It fit Abbey's personality. He peered back at his dad's black SUV parked near the door. Practical. A workhorse. Did that fit him even though it was his father's?

After he had unloaded Abbey's car and transferred her possessions to the house, he scanned the foyer. "Where's Gabe?"

"Exploring the living room. Don't tell Mrs. Ponder," Abbey said, and withdrew her leash from a bag and made her way into the room.

"Go on outside with Cottonball. I'll leave your manual wheelchair out there for when you all come back." Dominic followed his sister down the ramp to the SUV, then he took the bichon and placed her in the backseat.

As he was transferring Madi into the car, Abbey came out of the house with Gabe right next to her. She put the Lab in the back with Madi and Cottonball while he stuck the wheelchair in the back of the SUV in case it was needed.

When he rounded the front of the car to get into the driver's side, he met Abbey. "I know you asked me earlier on the phone about taking Madi to church. That's fine with me."

"Has Madison been to church much?"

"I don't know. We went once on Christmas Eve when I was visiting two years ago. My mother's faith was strong, and we went every week when she was alive. Dad stopped going after she died. A lot of things changed then." But so had Dominic, especially when he'd moved to Houston.

"How old were you when she died?"

"Twelve." His gaze roped hers. "Dad retreated for several years. I didn't know how to help him."

"Looking back with regret doesn't do much for me. There's no use beating yourself up over what you should have done. It sounds like your father finally got his life together. He married again and had a child."

Dominic frowned. "Yeah, he did."

Silence hovered between them.

Abbey cleared her throat. "I think it'll be good to get Madison out of the house a little now that she's starting to feel better. She seems to have more energy each day."

"I trust you. Use your judgment." When he said those words, part of him was surprised, because trust didn't come easy for him. He'd trusted his father and Susie and look what had happened.

As he moved past her, their arms brushed against each other. The brief contact stayed with him as he drove to the small airport where the company jet waited. The whole way there Madi talked to Gabe and Cottonball, telling them what she was seeing out the window as though they couldn't see for themselves.

He slanted a look at Abbey. She shifted toward him and caught him peering at her. The corners of her mouth tilted up.

"I hope everything goes all right in Houston," Abbey said, tucking her auburn hair behind her ears.

When he returned his attention to the road, he still felt her gaze on him. "So do I. I'm not sure what to say to the family tonight at the wake."

"The right words will come to you."

He wasn't so sure. After burying several close family members in his thirty-one years, he'd rather avoid funerals. He still hadn't come to terms with his father's and Susie's deaths. But he had a responsibility, and he wouldn't shirk his duties—not to his company and not to his sister.

He parked near the front of the small airport terminal and twisted around. "Kiddo, I'll be back by Sunday. If you need to talk to me, have Abbey call me. Okay?"

Madison nodded, her expression solemn.

She had been fine with him going when she heard Abbey and Gabe were staying with her, but from the storm-dark blue of her eyes, he still had reservations about leaving. "Are you sure you're all right?"

"Yes," his sister squeaked out. "Abbey explained this was important for you."

"Yes, but if you need me—"

"Go." Holding up the white dog, Madi buried her face against Cottonball.

Abbey opened her door and climbed from the SUV. "You heard her. Go."

He followed suit and skirted the front of the car to give Abbey the keys to the vehicle and house. "I shouldn't have let her ride to the airport. This can't be good for her to see. I should have thought of that. But she insisted on riding with you." The muscles in his neck and shoulders bunched up into tight knots.

"As Madison said, go. We'll be okay. Call when you reach Houston and talk to her. That'll make her feel better. I thought I would take her by my father's animal hospital while we're out. I'm going to surprise her. A tour might take her mind off you flying to Houston."

"She'll enjoy that." He took her hands, drawing closer to her. "Thanks for helping me." For so long he felt he'd done everything on his own, that any help he'd received was from paid employees. Foreign emotions had rocked his world of late.

"I'll be praying for you and the family."

"No one has said that to me in years." The very thought that she would unraveled some of the tension clenching him at having to leave his sister and attend Robert's funeral.

"Well, then it's about time someone did."

A strand of her red hair swept across her face and, before he realized it, he smoothed it back, his fingertips grazing across her cheek. The touch of her soft skin tingled through him, and he quickly lowered his arm to his side.

He cleared his throat. "I'd better go."

As he strode toward the building, he glanced over his shoulder to find Abbey where he'd left her, watching him. His world tilted off its axis. He needed to go to Houston, to be back in a familiar environment. He was losing all sense of who he was. Who he wanted to be. And somehow Abbey was the cause of that.

While Abbey parked in front of the animal hospital, one of her hands touched the cheek that Dominic had touched not twenty minutes ago. Her stomach still quivered from the brush of his fingers. She could almost imagine it was a caress, but that was a dangerous assumption.

She turned to see if Madison was still asleep. Not long after Abbey had left the airport, she'd glimpsed the child's eyes close, her body slumped partially against Gabe, with Cottonball sitting contently in her lap.

She would be with Madison for the next two or three days. What had possessed her to offer her services to

Dominic? At the moment, looking at the child's beautiful features, she couldn't separate Madison from Lisa in her mind. All the bittersweet memories flooded her as though the dam she'd shored up around them finally broke.

I shouldn't have done this. Sure, I wanted to help both Dominic and Madison. I always want to make things better for others—sometimes without thinking it through. Her father had called her a caregiver and hadn't really been surprised when she'd told him she wanted to be a social worker rather than a veterinarian.

Whether or not she should have offered to care for Madison while Dominic was gone, it was too late to change it. She would have to deal with her feelings, and his, when he returned to Cimarron City.

"We're here," Abbey finally said.

Waking up, Madison looked around. "Where are we?"

"I told my dad how much you like animals, and he thought you might enjoy a tour of his hospital. If you don't want to, that's okay. We can go back to the ranch."

"Are you kidding?" The girl sat up straight. "Are we taking Gabe and Cottonball inside, too? I don't want to leave them in the car."

"Of course. Gabe comes here a lot and knows how to behave. You can keep a hold on Cottonball. Do you think you can do that?"

"She's good. She'll stay in my lap."

"Then let's go. My dad is expecting us."

When Abbey brought the wheelchair around and moved Madison to it, the girl took Cottonball and held her against her. Abbey put Gabe on his leash, and they headed into the building. Inside, her father and several of the employees, including Emma, stood in the reception area waiting for Madison. A large sign hung across the doorway into the back read Welcome Madison.

Her dad, who wore a party hat and had a noisemaker, said, "We're so glad that you could come and see us today."

Her friend and vet hospital employee, Emma Langford, added, "We always like a chance to celebrate and show this place off."

Abbey's father blew into the noisemaker. Emma and the other two employees did the same, and in the background there was a chorus of dogs barking as though her dad had planned that.

Madison smiled from ear to ear, clapping and letting go of Cottonball.

The bichon jumped down and shot toward the doorway into the exam rooms and kennel area. Her dad tried to catch Cottonball, but she slipped through his legs. The barking increased to a din.

Madison slapped her hand over her mouth, her eyes huge. "I'm so sorry! I didn't mean to do that."

The child pushed herself off the seat of the wheelchair and tried to stand as if she wanted to chase after the dog. When she couldn't she plopped down, dropping her head.

Chapter Six

Abbey darted after Cottonball. She'd seen the fear on the dog's face when her dad had blown into the noisemaker. The sound had spooked her. In the hallway Abbey glanced both ways trying to decide which way the little dog had gone. The kennel was on the right, along with all the dogs barking. To the left were the exam rooms. She turned to the left, hoping Cottonball was seeking some quiet.

Her father came in as Abbey found the bichon under the chair in the second exam room. "I've learned today she's scared of loud noises." She picked up Cottonball and cradled the dog's shaking body against her chest. "You're okay, girl. Let's take you back to Madison. She's worried about you."

"I'm sorry, Abbey. I wanted to make the child feel special. Instead she's crying in the reception area. She thinks she did something wrong, and Cottonball is going to be hurt."

When Abbey heard her father's words, she hurried from the room and came to a halt near the doorway where Madison had wheeled herself.

Dominic's sister raised tear-filled eyes to Abbey. "You found her. I thought I had lost her because I didn't hold on to her tight enough. I promise I'll be careful next time. I don't want to lose another dog."

Abbey placed Cottonball in Madison's lap, then knelt in front of her. "You did fine. None of us knew Cottonball doesn't like loud noises. They don't bother Gabe or my other dogs."

Her father stopped behind Abbey. "Now that we know, we'll be more careful in the future with Cottonball. I'm Abbey's dad, Dr. Harris. I've heard a lot of nice things about you from my daughter. Are you ready for a tour of the animal hospital? We had a pregnant dog left on our doorstep this morning, and she delivered a few hours ago. She has three puppies."

"Why did someone leave her here and not come back for her?"

"Probably because they didn't want to deal with a litter of puppies. Sadly it happens sometimes." Her dad started walking toward the kennel area of the hospital.

As Abbey wheeled Madison behind her father while he showed the girl the play yard for the animals that were staying overnight, the large cages each pet had and the operating room, she remembered the desperation in Madison's voice when she'd said she couldn't lose another dog. She thought back to the death of her first pet. It had devastated her, and she'd never wanted to care for another animal. Her dad had taught her the best way to get over her grief was to give her love to another animal rather than hold it close to her heart. After that she started caring for another pet, then another. That might work with animals, but she didn't think it would work with people.

And yet, she ached to be a mother again. Was that why she was drawn to Madison in spite of the feelings and memories she evoked? Abbey wasn't quite sure.

Later that night a bark penetrated Abbey's sleep, followed by something cold against her hand, nudging it. She opened her eyes to find Gabe staring at her, a soft light from the hallway streaming through the doorway into the bedroom she was using next to Madison's.

Gabe yelped again.

"What's wrong?" Abbey sat up and swung her legs over the side of the bed. "Is it Madison?"

He barked once.

Abbey quickly rose and started for the hall. Gabe ran ahead of her. Something must have happened to Madison, or she was having one of the nightmares Dominic told her about. Abbey's heart pounded as she increased her pace.

When Abbey entered the child's room, Madison fought with her covers, moaning and sobbing. Cottonball stood watching the girl, trying to lick her cheek and console her.

Abbey rushed to the bed and scooped the child against her while switching on the lamp on the bedside table. She clutched Abbey, her sobs evolving into screams.

"Madison, wake up. Come on, honey."

Dominic's sister's eyes bolted open. She stared at Abbey without really seeing her for a long moment.

"Madi? Are you okay?"

She blinked, recognition dawning in her gaze. She clung to Abbey. "I heard Mom screaming. Daddy..." The girl shuddered.

"Hon, you're all right now. You're safe."

The sound of Madi crying shredded her composure, thrusting her back in time. The memories of holding her daughter while she cried in pain ripped off the scab over the wound of Lisa's death. Abbey felt the heartache again as though three years hadn't passed.

Suddenly Madi yanked away from her. "Where's Cottonball?" Her gaze fastened onto the bichon, still on her bed but nearby. She pulled her close while wrapped in Abbey's embrace. "I probably scared her."

"She knew you were having a hard time. She stayed right by you." Abbey combed Madi's hair behind her ears, then framed her face. "Do you want to talk about the nightmare? Maybe I can help you."

The little girl shook her head. "Can't. I want to forget it. I…" Tears again welled in her eyes.

Abbey quickly searched for a way to take Madi's mind off what had happened. "Do you know that Gabe must have heard you, and he got me up to come see if you were okay?"

"He did?" Madi glanced around for the Lab.

As if sensing she was searching for him, Gabe came closer, and when she held out her hand, he licked it.

Madi giggled. "That tickles." She patted both Gabe and the bichon. "I like Cottonball sleeping with me. Can Gabe stay in here, too?"

"Sure. In fact, I'll stay until you fall asleep, if you want."

"Yes. I don't like dreaming about the wreck."

"I know, honey. Here let me tuck you in again." Abbey straightened the sheets that looked like Madi had lost the battle with the covers. "There, is that better?"

The girl nodded, her mouth forming a big O as

she yawned. "You can lie down. There's room." Madi scooched over to give Abbey even more of the bed.

"Sometimes I used to stay with my daughter until she fell asleep. I'd start telling her a story, and before I could finish, she would be asleep." She couldn't seem to stop the wave of memories. This weekend might be harder than she thought it would be.

"Can you tell me a story? What was your daughter's favorite?"

Emotions jammed Abbey's throat. She swallowed hard, shifting away to blink the moisture from her eyes. *"The Princess and the White Rose."*

"Oh, that sounds good. What was the princess's name?"

"Rose. She prided herself on her gardens, working every day in them, even though her father, the king, didn't want her to. He wanted her to find a young man and get married."

Madi snuggled up against Abbey, her eyes sliding closed.

"Rose never wanted to get married. She was sure no man would understand her love of flowers, especially roses." Abbey peered at Dominic's sister. "Madi?"

The child didn't stir beside Abbey. She continued holding the girl while she recalled the last time she'd told Lisa the story—the day before she'd died. She couldn't do this. Madi reminded her too much of Lisa. They didn't look alike, but the two were connected in Abbey's mind.

When she was sure that Madi was sound asleep, Abbey left Gabe with the child and slipped out of the girl's room, too restless to go back to bed yet. She thought she would fix a cup of the tea that helped her relax when she was wound tight.

When she entered the kitchen, she found Mrs. Ponder sitting at the table sipping something from a mug. Abbey noticed the black kettle was on a burner. "Is there some hot water left?"

"Yes."

"May I use it and refill the kettle for you?"

"Help yourself. The water and kettle belong to Mr. Winters." As Abbey crossed to the stove, Mrs. Ponder asked, "You can't sleep, either?"

"No, Madi had a bad dream. Gabe woke me up so I could go comfort her."

"He did? He must be smart."

Abbey poured some hot water into a mug she found in the cabinet. "Gabe is sensitive to people's needs." Abbey turned with her tea and started to move toward the exit but decided not to. Instead, she took the chair across from Mrs. Ponder.

"I'm sure you've sensed I don't like dogs."

"I kind of got the feeling. Did you ever have a pet?"

"No," Mrs. Ponder said in an abrupt tone, then took a drink.

Silence descended. Abbey started to rethink her decision to stay.

"I was cornered by a boxer when I was seven," the housekeeper blurted out. "I still have scars from the bite marks on my arm." She pulled up her sleeve on her nightgown to reveal the evidence of the dog attack. "I've learned to keep my distance. I tolerated Zoe mostly because she was small and Madison adored her."

"I'm sorry. I've been bitten before, too."

"You have?"

"Yes. I was a teenager and helping my dad at his animal hospital. When I was assisting him in controlling an injured dog, the poodle bit me." Abbey sipped her tea and released a long breath as she felt herself unwind. "Do you have trouble sleeping, too?"

"Sometimes."

"After my daughter died and I couldn't sleep well, my mother shared some tea she used to help her sleep. It's a special green tea blend with chamomile. It relaxes me, and usually I'll fall asleep. I didn't like the sleeping pills my doctor prescribed for me."

"When did your daughter die?"

Abbey cupped her mug between her palms and stared at Mrs. Ponder. Surprised at the kind expression in her eyes, Abbey answered, "Three years ago."

"I had a son who died when he was a teenager. I think of him every day. A parent shouldn't have to lose a child."

"I'm sorry for your loss. It's never easy." In that moment, Abbey realized she would try to get to know Mrs. Ponder. Abbey understood her suffering. "What happened?"

"A motorcycle wreck. He lived for two days. What happened to your daughter?"

"She died when she was five from leukemia."

"I'm sorry."

"Me, too."

"Does that tea really help you? I've been trying various things and haven't found a remedy yet."

"Usually. Would you like to try some of mine? I have plenty."

"Sure. Why not? It can't be any worse than this—" Mrs. Ponder held up her cup "—which was advertised to help a person sleep. It hasn't, and I've been drinking it for a week." She made her way to the stove and fixed herself a cup of Abbey's tea.

When she retook her chair, Mrs. Ponder sipped her drink. "Mmm. There's a hint of banana in this."

"Yes. It surprised me, too. But a banana has tryptophan. It changes to melatonin and serotonin, which can aid in sleeping."

"I'm glad Mr. Winters was able to go to Houston. I've seen how worried he's been about his employees in Costa Sierra. He needed to attend the funeral."

As she talked with Mrs. Ponder, Abbey relaxed, whether it was from the tea or from the fact that, for the first time since she'd been in the house, Mrs. Ponder was personable. She never thought she'd feel a kinship with the woman who didn't like animals in her house, but she did. Abbey finished her tea and rose. "It was nice getting to know you. I'd better go up and check to make sure Madi has stayed asleep. Although I suspect if she hadn't, Gabe would have come down and gotten me."

"Hmm. That's interesting. He's really that sensitive to Madison's moods?"

"Yes. When I used to have nightmares after Lisa died, he'd wake me up and comfort me. There was something about petting him that always calmed me. I think that's what Madi is discovering."

"Good. She's gone through so much these past six months."

"I'll leave the tea down here. Take what you need. I have plenty." Abbey left the kitchen, thanking God for giving her a chance to see another side to Mrs. Ponder.

She might not have converted her into an animal lover, but at least now she knew how to connect with her.

"How is everything going with Madi?" With his cell phone against his ear, Dominic pushed to his feet behind his desk. Restless, he paced his Houston office, part of him wishing he was back at the ranch. But he had a duty to the people who worked for him, who depended on his company for their livelihood.

"She had another bad dream last night. Gabe woke me up, and I stayed with her until she fell asleep."

The concern and care in Abbey's voice soothed Dominic's guilt that he should be in Oklahoma rather than in Texas. It eased the uneasy feelings of being pulled into two different directions. "Did she scream out?"

"No, just wrestled with her covers and moaned."

"I usually don't know she's having a bad dream until she screams out. As I told you, I have a monitor in her room, but I've been so exhausted that I must sleep too soundly. So a dog like Gabe could alert me before it gets bad?"

"Possibly. He used to wake me up when I had nightmares."

"After your daughter's death?"

"Yes."

A wealth of unsaid emotion was bound up in that one-word answer. Dominic wished he could be there, not only for his sister, but for Abbey, too. He realized his sister was the same age as her daughter would have been if she'd lived. That couldn't be easy on Abbey, and yet she'd agreed to help him. "Then I may need to get a dog like Gabe. In six months Madi has only gone a couple of nights without waking up from bad dreams, and she never talks to me about them. I think it would help."

"I agree. I know a lady who trained Gabe to help me know when Lisa needed me at night. I can see if Emma has another dog like him."

"That would be great."

"I wish I could give you Gabe, but..." Her raspy voice faded into the silence.

"I wouldn't ask you to give up your dog. I know how special he is to you. You've done so much for us, Abbey. I wouldn't even know it was possible to have an animal to alert me like that."

"Emma, a veterinarian assistant at my dad's animal hospital, has a brother who was a soldier in the Middle East. He returned home with post-traumatic stress disorder. That's when she read up about the dogs that could help him and started training one for him."

"Thanks, Abbey. It's a great idea. I'll try to be home as early as I can. I've imposed on you long enough."

"Don't worry about that. We all need help from time to time. What kind of Christian would I be if I didn't offer to help you?" Madi said something to Abbey in the background. "Your sister has reminded me we're due at the nursing home soon, and she's ready to go with Cottonball and Gabe. See you soon. Bye."

When Abbey hung up, Dominic lowered the cell phone and glanced around his office, not really seeing anything. All he could picture was Abbey watching him entering the airport terminal, strands of her hair dancing about her face. An intensity had reached across the distance between them, tempting him to walk back to her and kiss her goodbye. He hadn't, but that was all he'd thought about on his flight down to Houston.

With a sigh, Dominic realized he'd moved over to stand at the window of his office high-rise in Houston. He stared at a landscape of buildings that he had become familiar with the past seven years. And for the first time he missed the green stretch of pastures when he peered out of a window at Winter Haven Ranch. There was something comforting when he looked at the sea of grasses and trees, occasionally dotted with horses or cattle grazing, even with all he had been handling lately.

Unhappy with his view, Dominic rotated around to take in his office that, until this morning, he hadn't set foot in for over six months. A massive oak desk dominated the large room, with a couch and two wing chairs on the right side, while on the left was a round table with six chairs for small meetings. He'd lived here six or seven days a week, often spending twelve or fourteen hours at work, dealing with one crisis after another. But nothing had prepared him to handle the situation he was in now—being guardian to his sister, who was hurting so much and keeping it all bottled up inside her.

When he heard her cry out in the night, he was there to hold her. But no amount of coaxing could get her to tell him what was bothering her so much that she would wake up screaming—even months after the accident. A counselor hadn't been able to help yet. Would a dog help Madi like Abbey thought? He'd heard of therapy dogs. He had to admit Gabe had made his sister laugh more than she ever had before.

A knock at the door pulled his attention back to what he'd returned to Houston to do. "Come in."

His CFO, Samuel, entered the office. "The department heads are here to meet with you in the conference room. They're especially eager to discuss the situation in Costa Sierra."

"Did you see the employees who were hostages at the funeral yesterday? I could see how hard the funeral was on them. Are we doing everything we can for them and their families?" The only burials worse than the one yesterday were Dominic's parents' funerals.

"We have them with the best counselors in Texas."

"I know. But the faster we can move our factory to the United States, the better I'll feel."

"We're looking at possible locations in Texas and the surrounding states first. I'll have a list of possibilities to you by the end of the month."

"In the meantime we need to fortify our security in Costa Sierra. I don't want anyone else kidnapped, no matter who they are." Dominic shuffled some papers on his desk until he found the ones he needed for the meeting.

"It's already being done. Dominic, we've worked together for years. Don't worry about the company. You need to be with your sister. Family comes first."

"And I'm keeping you from yours. How do you manage to have a wife and two sons and still do your job and mine?"

"I have a wife and two sons who are my life. I make sure I have quality time with them. That's more important than quantity. You just haven't found the right woman to give you a more important reason than work to live. Besides, the staff you've hired is excellent. They do their job, which makes mine much easier."

When he listened to his longtime friend, sadness engulfed Dominic. How had he let his life become so all consumed with work? Could he even change, especially now that he was responsible for Madi? Did he want to?

"You can't have Gabe. I've called dibs on him first." In the courtyard, Mr. Johnson waved his hand toward the bichon that Madi cradled in her lap. "You can have—what do you call her?"

"Cottonball." Madi answered, a twinkle in her gaze.

Mr. Johnson's eyes grew round. "Oh, no, they've found out you're here with Gabe."

Abbey turned around. Surprise streaked through her. The number of patients coming out into the courtyard had doubled since the last time she'd visited. This had been planned with Mr. Johnson as a quick outing for Madi on Saturday and an opportunity for the man to have some special one-on-one time with Gabe. It didn't appear that would be the case, and from the frown on Mr. Johnson's face, he wasn't too happy.

"This is *my* time," Mr. Johnson grumbled.

"I'll share Cottonball with them. You don't have to share Gabe."

"Well, well…" The old man flapped his mouth as though he didn't know what to say to Madi.

Abbey pressed her lips together to keep from laughing at the flabbergasted look on Mr. Johnson's face. She turned to the group moving toward them in walkers and wheelchairs. Two staff members accompanied these patients.

The small frail woman from Thursday shook her finger at Mr. Johnson. "Shame on you for not telling us Abbey was bringing Gabe and that other dog to see us."

"*Us?* They came to see *me*." Beet-red, Mr. Johnson thumped his chest.

"My lands, how can you hog both dogs?" another eightysomething lady muttered. "Abbey, we need more."

"Yes, Mrs. Parks, I'll have to check with Mrs. Rosen if I can bring more than one or two." She'd snuck in Cottonball the other day, but she'd seen the look the director had given her.

The nurse's aide from Thursday pushed a patient over to where Abbey stood with Madi.

"My supervisor said something to Mrs. Rosen about how happy the patients on her wing were when they came in from being with Gabe and this dog." She waved her hand toward the bichon as Madi passed her to the wheelchair patient with short black hair.

Madi glanced at the nurse's aide. "I call her Cottonball."

"What a cute name." The older woman took Cottonball, shaking so badly that Madi reached and helped to place the dog in the lady's lap. "I used to have a white dog. Heinz 57 breed."

"What's that?" Madi asked.

"A huge mix of many different kinds of dogs, but he was so sweet. I miss him."

"I had a dog named Zoe. I miss her."

The black-haired woman patted Madi's arm. "We have to remember all the good times we had with them. I won't ever forget Butch."

"I won't forget Zoe, either." Madi rolled her chair closer to the lady.

That was the first time Madi had ever talked about Zoe dying. She still wouldn't talk about her parents, even when she'd woken up again last night, this time calling out for her mom over and over. She wouldn't say anything to Abbey other than asking if she would stay with her until she fell asleep.

After about fifteen minutes, Mr. Johnson relented and let one of the four men in the courtyard take Gabe. Using his walker, the gentleman helped pass Gabe from one patient to the next.

Madi grinned at Mr. Johnson. "That's so sweet what you did. Look at their smiles."

Mr. Johnson harrumphed. "Yeah, but I'd still like to have more quality time with Gabe."

Hearing Mr. Johnson planted the seed of an idea in Abbey's mind. She needed to think about how it could work, but once she figured out some of the details she intended to come back and see Mrs. Rosen. In the meantime, she hoped others would tell the director how effective the dogs were for the patients.

Later, on the ride back to the Winter Haven Ranch, Madi chattered the whole way about the different people. "The only grandparent I met was my mom's dad. He lives in Florida and came for the funeral. He was very sad. I didn't like seeing him cry." ·

"I know what you mean, but crying is a form of emotional release. We need to, sometimes."

"I've cried over Zoe."

Yes, but have you over your parents? Dominic told Abbey he hadn't seen his sister cry once about her mom and dad. What was she keeping to herself? Dominic said the counselor Madi was seeing thought the girl wasn't dealing with something. Maybe it was the crash itself, but if it wasn't that, what was she trying to avoid?

"For the longest time after my daughter died, I wouldn't even say her name out loud. I wouldn't admit that she had died until my father had our pastor come over to my house. He planted himself in my living room and said he wouldn't leave until he'd really talked with me."

"How long did he stay?"

"All day. I even tried to ignore him. But I couldn't. He helped me with my chores, chatting about things that were unimportant. He had lunch and dinner with me. I finally told him he had to leave."

"Did he?"

"No, he looked at me with the kindest eyes and asked me if I was ready to talk about Lisa. He wanted to hear about her life." Abbey turned into the ranch's drive and brought the SUV to a stop, her body trembling at the onslaught of memories deluging her when she thought of the four-hour conversation with her pastor. She'd laughed, cried, got angry and even rejoiced at the end that Lisa was with Jesus and not in pain anymore. She swallowed the lump in her throat and said, "So anytime you want to talk about your parents and some of the fun times you had with them, I'll listen."

Through the rearview mirror Abbey saw Madi drop her head until her chin touched her chest. She waited a few minutes, but the girl didn't say anything so Abbey put the car into Drive and headed for the house.

Saturday night Abbey left her bedroom to fix a cup of tea before turning in for the night. First, she would check on Madi to make sure she was sleeping okay. Since she had put her to bed only an hour ago, she should be all right because her nightmares usually didn't occur until later in the night.

As she approached the girl's room, Abbey heard talking. She slowed and listened to the child.

"If I don't sleep, I don't dream, but I'm getting sleepy." Her voice dragged with each word Madi said.

Abbey inched toward the bedroom, the door opened partially the way Madi liked it. Abbey peeked inside. The girl had both dogs on her bed, Gabe stretched out on one side while Cottonball was on the other. She cuddled the smaller animal against her chest as she stroked the Lab.

"I can't keep my eyes open any longer. I don't want to dream about the crash. I don't want to hear my mom…." Cottonball snuggled closer to the child's face and licked her on the cheek. "She screamed…." Her eyes slid closed.

Abbey crept into the room. The pain she heard in Madi's voice brought tears to Abbey. Through blurry vision she saw the girl's eyes pop open while she sucked in a deep breath.

"Can't sleep," Madi murmured.

Abbey crossed to the bed, her gaze linking with Madi's. "I thought you'd be asleep by now with all we did today."

Madi gave her a tired grin. "It was fun except for my exercises."

"Well, it's time to go to sleep. We'll be up early tomorrow so we can get ready for church."

"I know, but…" Madi sighed.

"But what?"

"I don't want to sleep." Madi yawned.

"Why are you fighting it?" She prayed the child would confide in her.

"I just don't."

"Are Cottonball and Gabe keeping you up?"

Madi shook her head. "I'll try to sleep."

"Sleep is important to our bodies. When you're rested, you heal faster, and I know you want to feel better."

"Yes." Another yawn escaped Madi's mouth, and her eyes closed. "You aren't taking them away, are you?" She nestled into the covers.

"No, honey. Cottonball and Gabe will be right here with you."

"Good."

Abbey waited ten minutes before she left Madi. If there was a problem, Gabe would find her downstairs. When she entered the kitchen, Mrs. Ponder stood at the sink rinsing out her mug.

The housekeeper swung around. "I thought you'd fallen asleep. I was going to bed."

"Madi was trying to stay up. I didn't want to leave until she was sleeping."

Since that first night, she and Mrs. Ponder had shared a cup of tea and talked before going to bed. Although there still was a certain formality between them, she had come to respect the woman and what she had gone through. She had shared the death of her son with Abbey, and Abbey had shared Lisa's death with Mrs. Ponder.

"I can stay if you want to talk." Mrs. Ponder dried her hands on a dish towel.

"No, that's okay. I think I'll take my tea upstairs. I'm in the middle of reading a good book."

"Then good night. See you in the morning." Mrs. Ponder headed toward her suite of rooms on the first floor.

Abbey turned on the burner with the kettle on it, then wandered around the kitchen until she stopped at the large bay windows that overlooked the backyard. A security light glowed in several places around the house and illuminated the pool and the garden of flowers in full bloom.

When the security system began beeping, indicating someone had come in or gone out, she whirled around and hurried to see what was going on. Rounding the corner into the hallway that led to the foyer, she literally ran into Dominic.

Chapter Seven

"What are you doing here?" Abbey asked as Dominic grasped her by the arms, steadying her.

One of his eyebrows rose. "I live here."

"I mean now. It's late, and I thought you were returning tomorrow afternoon." His hands still clasped her arms, and the feel of them on her sent her heartbeat speeding.

"I pushed everything forward as much as possible. I didn't want to be away too long." He finally released her and rubbed the five-o'clock shadow along his jawline. "I've been up since 5:00 a.m. trying to get finished." He cocked a grin. "I know I should have called, but I wanted to surprise you and Madi. I was hoping to get back before she went to bed."

The curve of his mouth and the scent of his spicy aftershave enticed her to remain near him in the hallway. But the shriek of the kettle went off.

"You didn't miss Madi by much." Abbey turned toward the kitchen, glancing over her shoulder at him. "I found her talking with Cottonball and Gabe, trying to stay awake. She told them she didn't want to fall asleep and dream."

"Then how did you get her to sleep?" Dominic trailed her into the kitchen.

She removed the kettle from the burner. "I told her how important it is to rest her body. I also assured her Cottonball and Gabe would be right there with her. But I don't think that's what really got her to sleep. I wish my sage advice was what did the trick, but I think it was because we did a lot today and she was worn-out."

"How did she like the nursing home? As much as your dad's animal hospital?"

Holding up the kettle, she asked, "Do you want some tea?"

He shook his head. "I'm a coffee drinker."

"She enjoyed herself, but her favorite place is the animal hospital. She's already asked me if she could go back and visit the puppies born a few days ago. So how did your trip go?" Being in his kitchen as if she belonged there added a hint of nervousness to her voice that she hoped he didn't hear.

Dominic sank into a chair at the table. "We're definitely looking into moving the factory in Costa Sierra to a place in the United States. It'll be an exhausting search for the perfect place but necessary."

Abbey sat across from Dominic, seeing the tired lines in his face, the loosened tie about his neck and the finger-tousled hair as though he'd been wrestling with something. "Why don't you build the factory here in Cimarron City? This is your hometown. You have a ranch here and this area could use the infusion of jobs."

For a long moment he stared at her, a blank expression on his face. Had she overstepped her boundaries again? What did she know about a big company like his? She was sure there were a lot of considerations concerning a factory move. "Forget I said anything."

A smile broke out on his face. "No, that's brilliant. I was trying to find a place within a couple of hundred miles of Houston, but I really don't have to. My headquarters can be moved here, if I want."

Abbey lifted her mug to her mouth and sipped. She loved seeing his smile, from the dimples in his cheeks to the tiny lines at the corners of his eyes to the glittering fire in his blue eyes. "Sometimes we're so close to a problem that we don't see a solution before us."

"I know that my profit could be more if I continued to open new factories in other countries rather than the United States, but I've often been someone who goes against the grain. I have several factories in Texas and Louisiana, but three years ago, we were looking at ways to increase the company's profit and built our next factory abroad."

"Is your company publicly owned?"

"No, and I'm the major shareholder."

"I know this sounds like a cliché, but money isn't everything."

"I'm discovering that since coming back to the ranch. But with that said, my company must make money to stay in business. I might be able to use the fact my products are made in the U.S.A. to my advantage. Up until recently we'd been looking to build another factory in the Far East. Maybe it's time to rethink those plans, too." He reached toward her and clasped her hand. "Thank you for helping with Madi but also for suggesting Cimarron City."

She wasn't sure what was relaxing her more, the

tea or his touch. All she wanted to do was melt against the back of the chair and stare into his handsome face. When he slipped his hand away from hers, a jolt shook her. What was she doing? He had enough to cope with, and she certainly didn't want to become involved in a relationship. She was still trying to work herself through what her husband had done. Recently, she'd realized she hadn't come to terms with Lisa's death three years ago as much as she had thought. And rage toward Peter simmered in the pit of her stomach, just waiting to rise to the surface. Again she questioned the wisdom of getting more deeply involved with Dominic and his eight-year-old sister.

Abbey rose. "I'd better…"

He came to his feet, too, the action disrupting her thoughts. He moved around the table until he stood inches from her. Her throat went dry. His gaze held her as though his arms were around her. "I'm glad to be back here. I can't believe I'm saying that. There was a time I thought I would never return to this ranch. Now it's mine. You're part of the reason for those feelings. I wouldn't have felt comfortable leaving Madi with just anyone. Please let me pay you for your services. I know we talked about this before, but you spent two and a half days with my sister. I know how time-consuming she can be—"

Anger washed over her. She pushed past him. "I didn't do it for you. I did it for Madi. I don't want your money. I thought I made that clear. Maybe you've been gone too long from Cimarron City, but here people often help people without putting a price on it."

"You took a day off from work. One of your vacation days. At least let me pay you for that."

All the warm, fuzzy feelings that had swept through her earlier were gone, replaced with disappointment, irritation and—she couldn't even decide what else she was feeling at the moment. She clenched her hands and started for the staircase, intending to pack and leave now that Dominic was home.

When she placed her foot on the first step, his hand clasped her arm and halted her progress. "I didn't mean to insult you. I'm used to paying for what I need or want." He turned her toward him. "Please accept my apology."

She glared at him, trying to figure out why she was so angry. No, *hurt* by him. She'd thought they were friends. Friends helped each other without expecting anything in return.

A bark behind her sent her rotating toward the staircase and fixing her gaze on Gabe. "Madi is having a nightmare." She hurried up the steps with Dominic right behind her.

Passing her, he went into his sister's room first and sat on the bed as he leaned forward and woke her up. "Madi, wake up. It's a bad dream. That's all."

His sister's eyelids slowly lifted. "Dominic, you're home."

"Yep, couldn't stay away from you too long."

"I'm glad you're back." Madi threw her arms around Dominic.

Abbey backed away from the bed. This was a good time for her to leave. Five minutes later she took her suitcase downstairs and set it by the front door. She couldn't leave without at least telling him she was going. Plus, she needed to decide what to do about Cottonball,

Gabe and the plans she'd made with Madi for tomorrow morning.

When she returned to Madi's room, Dominic held his sister in his arms, whispering over and over she was okay while Madi cried. Abbey backed away. She heated up water in the kitchen, fixed herself some tea, then took a seat on the bottom of the stairs to wait for Dominic.

Spending time with Madi these past few days had made her realize what she'd lost all over again. She had to deal with feelings she'd tried to bury for three years. And she couldn't do that. Yet how could she not be involved in Madi's life? She cared for her—and for Dominic. He was grasping for what to do with this new situation. She knew what it was like to have your old life ripped from your hands and given a new one—one you didn't want.

She cupped the mug and sipped the hot tea, relishing its warmth. What did she want to do? She liked her job at the hospital, especially because she was helping others through difficult times, but what she really enjoyed the most was bringing Gabe or one of her other therapy dogs to see patients at the hospital or the nursing home. She remembered the laughter and smiles she'd seen earlier today from the patients at the home. One man had enjoyed tossing the ball for Gabe to retrieve. Mrs. Parks had been in charge of Cottonball as the bichon was passed from one person to the next. She made sure everyone got the same amount of time with the dog. Next week she would pay Mrs. Rosen another visit. Patients, family members and staff had been telling the director how nice it was to have an animal at the nursing home. But was it enough?

Lord, I have to give this to You. If You want the dogs to be part of the nursing home, please smooth the way with Mrs. Rosen.

"I wondered where you'd gone." Dominic's deep, husky voice came to her from the second-floor landing.

She saw him descend the stairs and sit next to her.

"That was rough. She was glad to see me but wondered where you were."

"I'm sorry. I didn't want to interfere. I went to pack my bag."

"Pack your bag?"

Staring at her luggage, she gestured toward the front door. "Yeah, I figured with you home, I should leave."

He placed two fingers under her chin and turned her head so she looked into his eyes, full of weariness. The past few days were written all over his face. "First, you are not interfering. I know in an emergency I could have left her with Mrs. Ponder, but that would have been hard on Madi and Mrs. Ponder. Madi told me how much fun she's been having with you and Cottonball and Gabe. She's enjoyed having an outing every day. I should have realized she needed more activity. When we went out, we went to the hospital or doctor's office mostly."

"She's been recovering from a trauma. Her body is just beginning to really heal itself. I found with Lisa, even when she was sick, she needed as normal a life as possible. Madi missed the last five months of school because of her injuries. She's been missing her friends lately."

"Why hasn't she said anything to me?"

"She didn't tell me. She told Cottonball, but with me, she acted like it wasn't that important that her friends have seemed to move on. What's happened to her has thrown her into a whole new life. Like you."

His eyebrows dipped down. "Why does she talk to Cottonball and not me?"

"She just sits there and listens. That's safe. Madi is wrestling with so many strange emotions. It's better to use Cottonball or Gabe as a sounding board. They don't talk back or judge."

"What's she going to do when you take them home with you?"

"I need to talk to you about that. I'll leave both dogs here tonight and pick them up tomorrow, unless you want to keep Cottonball. How do you feel about having her here permanently?"

"I know Madi was upset about losing Zoe. That's the only grief she's ever really displayed openly, other than at the funeral for her parents. And even then she only cried during the memorial. As I've mentioned to you, I've tried talking to her about her dad and mom, but she doesn't say much to me or her counselor. It's very frustrating."

"I know. Maybe she's grieving Zoe's death as a symbol for her parents, too. When you talk about a person being dead out loud, that makes it more real, and right now with all the injuries and surgeries she suffered, she isn't ready to deal with that."

"Makes sense." Leaning forward, he propped his elbows on his thighs and clasped his hands together, staring at the marble floor of the foyer. "Even I have a hard time believing they're gone. I think Cottonball would be a good addition to our family. I want to do everything I can to help Madi."

"You remember me mentioning Emma, my friend

who trained Gabe? I could talk to her about finding a dog for Madi to sense her nightmares and come and alert you, or she can train Cottonball to do that. There are several options you need to consider, maybe talk it over with your sister." She knew Gabe would be wonderful with Madi, too, but Abbey couldn't let him go. He meant too much to her. "And in the meantime, until you can get a dog like that, I can loan Gabe to you, if you want. If I can use him when I visit the patients at the hospital and the nursing home. Actually, Madi might like to go to the home again. She and Mrs. Parks seemed to hit it off."

"Training Cottonball would probably be the best. She seems like a smart little dog. And I won't turn down the offer of Gabe. If I can stop the nightmares before they get too bad, it helps Madi recover faster and go back to sleep. She needs her rest. The doctor stressed that." He pressed his fingertips into his temples. "How do you know you're doing what's right for a loved one?"

"You don't always."

He slanted a glance toward her. "I'm sorry about offering to pay you for staying with Madi. This is all new to me, and I'm bound to make a few mistakes along the way. Probably a lot. I never envisioned myself having a child depend on me."

"You never thought about getting married and having children?" It had to be the exhaustion causing her to ask that question. She averted her gaze and wished she could retract it.

"Once, but it didn't work out, and since then I've thrown myself into work. I've been so busy these past ten years that I didn't ever stop to think about that. I guess it's a moot point now. How about you? Ever thought of getting remarried, and having more children?"

"A month ago I would have said no. But being around Madi reminds me of what I'm missing. It hasn't always been easy. But I don't want to go through that kind of pain again." She stole a look at Dominic as she revealed what she had come to realize these past few days.

"I can certainly understand that. After the woman I loved married someone else, I decided I didn't want to depend on anyone else for my happiness."

This was the first time she'd realized he'd planned to marry someone. "And your company gives you that happiness?" She enjoyed her work, but it could never replace the joy she'd felt being a wife and mother.

"The truth?"

She locked gazes with him. "Always. What good is it to tell yourself a lie?" She'd told herself plenty of lies once upon a time. Especially the big lie that once Lisa got well, she would mend her marriage. But her child hadn't gotten well, and her husband had gotten tired of waiting.

"It used to make me happy. Seeing the company grow. Giving people a chance to work with decent wages. But now, something's missing, and I don't know what."

"Is it because of what happened in Costa Sierra?"

"Not really. It began even before my dad and Susie died. Oh, I went through the motions of going into work and doing my best because people depended on me, but I couldn't deny the emptiness I felt."

She understood exactly what he was talking about. Lisa had taken part of Abbey's heart when she died.

She hadn't been able to totally mend it—wasn't sure she ever could.

"I was devastated and dealing with a lot even before he walked out on our marriage."

"When did it happen?"

"Right before Lisa died."

"Your husband left you while your daughter was ill?"

"Yes."

"What kind of man was he?" Fury coated each word.

"One who wanted more from me than I could give at that time. We'd had Lisa because I wanted a child. I don't think he ever really did."

"But he walked away from his ill child?" He shook his head.

"He came to see her some, but he never liked to deal with people being sick. He couldn't even tolerate getting sick himself. I know I should forgive him and let it go. I can't change the past. But I can't let the anger go, or forgive him for what he'd done."

"I don't blame you. That's a lot to handle."

"After my marriage fell apart and my daughter passed away, I was struggling. I finally went to my pastor and actually got angry with him. Why was God doing those things to me? I'd lost my daughter and my husband, two of the people I was closest to. What had I done to make God so angry with me?"

"What did he say?"

"I hadn't done anything wrong. God wasn't angry with me. On the contrary, God loves me, warts and all."

"That's what my grandma used to say to me. That no matter what, God loves me."

"She's right. My pastor went on to tell me that there's no guarantee that we won't suffer even if we believe in

God. But what *is* guaranteed is that the Lord is always with us through our suffering. We aren't alone. He is still here with me. God is love. He's hope."

Dominic twisted his hands together. "I haven't been to church since I left home, and then I only went occasionally with a friend, after my mother died."

"That was something else I needed to talk with you about. Madi was looking forward to going with me tomorrow morning. I'd still like to take her, and you're welcome to come, too."

He dropped his arms to his sides and pushed himself up. "Let me think about it. In spite of what your pastor and my grandma have said, I'm not too sure God is real happy with me."

"May I still take Madi?"

"Of course. I don't want her to be disappointed, and I know how much getting her out and involved with others is good for her."

Abbey rose. "Then I'll see you all tomorrow. If you decide to go with us, our church is casual."

As she headed toward her bag, Dominic grabbed her suitcase before she could. "I'll walk you to your car."

The night enveloped her in its warm arms. She peered up at the dark midnight sky and saw thousands of glittering stars sprinkled across the blackness. Abbey inhaled a deep breath of the air, scented with earthy smells. "It's beautiful out here."

"And quiet. When I'm at the ranch, I think it's possible to have a slower-paced life, until I go back in the house and see all the work I still have to do. It's not as easy to run a large company here as in my office in Houston. But I'm getting used to videoconferencing with my staff."

"I can't believe I'm saying this, but change can be good. Maybe you needed to come home to the ranch."

"And do what my father wanted? No way. This ranch was his, not mine."

Determination and anger entwined through his voice, making Abbey wonder why he felt that way. What had happened to drive Dominic away from here? "But it's yours now. Are you thinking of selling it?"

"I don't know. There was a time I loved this place, and I know that Madi does. I can't take her away from Winter Haven right now. We'll stay at least until she gets back on her feet."

"Then move to Houston?" Abbey stopped at her car and unlocked the trunk.

Dominic hefted the bag into it. "Maybe." After slamming the lid down, he shifted toward her, his face visible in the soft glow from the security light nearby. "I'm not used to being so indecisive."

"And that upsets you?"

"Frustrates me more than upsets me. I'm used to making the decisions and coming up with ways to carry them out."

Abbey thought of a plan that she'd been kicking around for the past few months. "I have to stew about something and look at it from all sides. Sometimes it drives me crazy that I can't just say yes I'm going to do this or no I'm not."

"It sounds like you're doing that now."

"Yeah, I think there's a need for therapy and service dogs in this area. There are a couple of us who have therapy dogs and go to different places with them, but there aren't enough to go around. More and more residents at Shady Oaks want to be involved."

"So what do you want to do about it?" He leaned back against the car, crossing his legs.

"Start some kind of organization to connect dogs with people in need. I have a name—Caring Canines—but not much else."

"What about your job at the hospital?"

Abbey chewed her lower lip. "Now you see my problem. I still have to make a living, and, frankly, I'm not sure how to go about setting up an organization. My expertise is social work and counseling."

"Sounds like you need help."

She nodded.

"I might be able to help you."

His words took her by surprise. She sucked in a deep breath, then slowly exhaled. "Really? But you have so much going on in your life." She was trying to figure out how to spend less time with him, not more. He intrigued her, but she didn't want to get involved with anyone.

"Sometimes I'd like to have a diversion, especially now that Madi is home and won't have any more operations. If I don't see the inside of a hospital again, that would be great."

She laughed. "I'd better not say that or I'd starve."

"I doubt that. You're resourceful. Besides, I wouldn't let you starve."

The intensity in his voice caused her stomach to flip-flop. "Good to know. I'd better say good-night."

"You don't need to leave. I'd rather you not drive home this late."

She moved toward the driver's side door and opened it. "I'm a big girl. I've been doing it for years. I'll be fine." She slipped behind the steering wheel before she changed her mind. It was one thing to stay at the ranch when he was gone. Totally different when he was here.

He shut her door and motioned for her to roll the window down. When she did, he bent closer and asked, "What time does Madi need to be ready tomorrow morning?"

"I'll be by at ten. We'll go to the late service. Afterward, they have light snacks and a chance to talk to others. We may stay for that if she wants to."

"She'll be ready. Good night." He straightened and stepped back from the car.

As she drove away, she prayed he would come with her and his sister to church. She wanted to spend time with him, even though she knew there were so many reasons they weren't right for each other. First, he had too much on his mind to be interested in her. Second, she wasn't looking for a relationship—with any man. Third, with all that had been happening lately with Shady Oaks, and with Madi, she needed to turn her attentions to moving ahead with Caring Canines.

Dominic followed the sight of Abbey's taillights as she headed toward the highway. He recalled when Susie had given him his engagement ring back with little explanation other than it wasn't working out for them. He'd been stunned, and had wondered what signals he'd missed to warn him she hadn't wanted to marry him after all.

Probably much like how Abbey had felt when her husband had left her while Lisa was so sick. Was that what drew him to Abbey—they were in the same place, holding on to their anger? Why couldn't life be simple? He tried to rid himself of his animosity toward his father and Susie, but he couldn't seem to let it go. It clung to him like a second skin.

He'd come close just now to telling Abbey about why he'd left Winter Haven all those years ago. But he was glad he hadn't. With Abbey he found himself telling her things he'd never told anyone else. She was so easy to talk to. Well, he was a private person, and he never wanted to share himself again like he had with Susie. Look where it had gotten him.

He strode toward the deck, scanning the pastures surrounding the house. At one time his dream had been the same as his father's, to run the ranch. He stared out into the darkness. That all changed the day his father came to him with Susie to announce they planned to get married. The betrayal cut deep. He'd thought he'd forgiven his father. But he hadn't. And he knew now he hadn't forgiven Susie, either.

He was interested in Abbey. She brought a breath of fresh air into his stale life, but because of what Susie had done to him, he'd vowed he'd never let someone hurt him like that ever again. Abbey deserved the best. She'd gone through so much three years ago, and he never wanted to hurt her. How did he move on?

He gripped the post next to him and tried to calm the sudden flood of rage sweeping through him. *Madi should have been his daughter, not his sister.* He hadn't thought about that in a long time, not since Madi had been a baby.

Lord, if You're there, what do I do?

Chapter Eight

Sunday afternoon after church, Madi held on to a pole in the golf cart used as a form of transportation around the ranch. "A picnic. This is gonna be fun."

Abbey smiled at the little girl. "It's not too bumpy?"

"No, I'm holding on good. Is Cottonball all right?"

Abbey glanced down at the dog she had on her lap. "She likes this adventure. Great suggestion, Dominic, and I love the transportation."

"I can't wait until I can ride Spice again. Then we can do this a lot." Madi clapped her hands. "Look. Gabe is keeping up with us."

"This is good for him. He doesn't get to run like this much. I've been so busy I haven't gone jogging with him lately."

Dominic laughed. "I'm glad I'm not the only one who's neglected their exercise. I hadn't even thought about it until you said something."

"I think it's understandable when life gets crazy. Do you like to ride horses?" Abbey relished the light breeze blowing her hair, the scent of a field that had been mowed recently.

"Yes, but I haven't in years. I used to participate in rodeos," Dominic said.

"You did?" Madi asked from the backseat. "Like Dad?"

"Yes, I learned from the best. You know he was a champion for several years when he was younger."

"Yeah, he would tell me some of his stories. I'm still not sure I would sit on a horse that would try to buck me off."

"I'll tell you a secret, Madi. I wouldn't do it now, either. But I did when I was eighteen, and I had my fair share of crashing defeats. I'd be sore for days." Dominic caught Abbey's attention. "How about you? Ever fallen off a horse?"

"No, but then I've only ridden docile old mares."

"That was Mom. She didn't like to ride anything that went faster than a walk. I used—to ride rings…" Madi's voice vanished on the wind.

Abbey peered back. The girl stared at the pasture on her right-hand side. "It's nice to think of the good times, Madi."

The child shifted her attention to Abbey. "I know. It's just that she won't get to anymore. Do you think they ride horses in Heaven?"

Dominic pulled up under a large elm tree near a pond and stopped.

"I never thought about that. Anything is possible with the Lord, so who knows." Abbey climbed from the golf cart and went around to the back to grab a blanket to spread on the ground.

"Maybe I should ask Pastor John about that. I liked church today," Madi said as she threw her arms around Dominic's neck, and he lifted her from the seat.

While Abbey fixed the blanket, Dominic carried Madi to her and gently placed his sister on the woolen material. "I'll get our picnic basket. I don't know about you two gals, but I'm starved."

"Yes. Those cookies after church weren't enough." Madi adjusted herself on the blanket.

"Then you should have eaten your breakfast." Dominic headed for the golf cart.

"You didn't eat before church?"

Madi shook her head. "I was nervous."

"Why?" Still holding Cottonball with one arm, Abbey sat across from Madi.

"I didn't know what to expect with my friends."

"From what I saw after the service, they were really glad to see you." Sitting with Dominic and Madi was a wonderful way to end a long weekend spent at the ranch. Dominic going to church with them this morning had been the highlight.

"I know. They hadn't forgotten me."

"You? No way. You're too special to forget." Abbey settled Cottonball next to Madi and staked her leash into the ground. "Just in case she decides to run after a bird or rabbit."

Madi pointed to Gabe sniffing the dirt under an oak tree nearby. "What about him?"

"He'll come to me when I whistle. He's trained. Cottonball isn't yet."

Dominic set the basket near Abbey, then took a seat. "I have to agree with Madi. Those cookies didn't satisfy my hunger either, and I ate breakfast. What did Mrs. Ponder fix for us?"

Abbey lifted the lid and peeked inside the brown woven basket. "I'm not sure. The food is in containers."

She withdrew one and passed it to Dominic, then passed another to Madi, and then took the last one out. She pried the top off to reveal sandwiches—lots of them. Chuckling, she showed Dominic and his sister. "She definitely doesn't want us to starve."

"Look at this. Cherry Jell-O with fruit and nuts in it. I love that." Madi grinned from ear to ear.

"And Mrs. Ponder knows that. I've got German potato salad. A favorite of mine." Dominic placed his plastic container in the middle along with the other food.

After Abbey handed everyone paper plates, utensils and bottles of tea, they all dug in, no one speaking for five minutes.

When Madi had eaten half a sandwich and part of her Jell-O, she asked, "Can I go with you to church next week, too?"

Abbey glanced at Dominic, not sure how to answer the child, but he was busy eating his potato salad. She wanted to say yes, but he was Madi's guardian. Finally Abbey said, "It's up to your brother."

"Dominic? Can I?"

"What? Oh, sorry. That's fine with me."

"Will you go, too?" his sister asked, and then took a bite of her sandwich.

Score one for Madi, Abbey thought, then realized that would mean they would be going together again if he said yes. She wasn't doing a good job of staying away from him.

"Well…"

"Please, Dominic. You liked Pastor John. You said so. He's funny." Madi used her pleading tone accompanied with her sad-eyed look.

Abbey resisted laughing.

"Sure. I'll go with you two. In fact, Abbey, we'll come by your house and pick you up."

Cheering, Madi clapped, perking Cottonball up.

Gabe even barked and trotted over to the blanket and sat, his gaze fixed on Abbey.

"You will not get any of this food, Gabe, so quit begging."

Madi produced a tennis ball, saying, "I'll distract him," and then she threw it.

While Gabe hurried after it, they finished up, and Abbey began to put the containers back into the basket. He trotted to Madi and dropped the ball in her lap.

"Now he'll expect you to play with him." Abbey rose and retrieved the hula hoop. "Remember I said I would show you some of his tricks besides sitting, lying down and shaking hands?"

"Oh, good. I've been teaching Cottonball to sit, and she's doing that."

Dominic's cell phone chimed. "I thought I turned that off." He pulled it out and checked who was calling. "I'd better take this. Samuel wouldn't call me on a Sunday unless it was important." He walked away from them.

Madi frowned. "I wonder what's wrong."

"Probably nothing. Okay, are you ready to be entertained?" Abbey asked, taking the child's attention off her brother because she could see his body tensing.

Dominic clicked off with Samuel and stood under the oak tree about forty feet from Abbey and Madi, struggling to compose himself before returning to them. The situation in Costa Sierra would only end when his company was completely gone. At the moment he couldn't think clearly. He'd gotten little sleep the night before because Madi had woken twice from a nightmare. He'd needed to rest after such an intense time in Houston. Once he'd assured her that both Cottonball and Gabe were with her, she finally drifted back to sleep.

But he hadn't. He'd nodded off in a chair in Madi's bedroom and came awake maybe two hours later with a sore neck, unable to go back to sleep.

This hectic pace had to stop or—

"Everything okay?" Abbey asked from behind him.

He hadn't even heard her approaching. The concern on her face made him feel he wasn't quite so alone. Looking around, he discovered that Madi had fallen asleep on the blanket. "I didn't think it would take much to wear her out. She had another nightmare after you left last night."

"She told me while you were parking the car at the church. I tried to get her to talk about it, but she clammed up."

"The same with me. I'm not sure what to do about it anymore. I keep wondering if something besides Dad and Susie dying is going on."

"Have you tried sharing how their deaths have affected you?"

Her question rumbled around in his mind as he tried to figure out how to answer her. Finally he said, "I don't know how to tell her that." *Because I'm feeling more than sorrow.*

"Practice on me, if you want."

"No."

Abbey's neutral expression morphed into a frown. "I'm sorry. I'm intruding." She pivoted and headed toward the blanket.

"Abbey, wait." He closed the space between them and turned her toward him. "The reason I said no is because I don't know what to say. My feelings are— complicated."

"I understand complicated."

"No, you don't." What happened between his dad and him didn't occur every day.

"You had a different vision for your life than your dad did. I didn't do what my father had wanted, either. He'd pictured me becoming a vet and going into practice with him. For a time I toyed with that because I love animals, but after a summer spent working for him, I realized I couldn't handle seeing so many injured animals. I wasn't tough enough to be a vet."

"There's nothing wrong with that. I don't think I could, either. Plus, I hated science in school." Could he redirect the conversation away from him and his mixed emotions concerning his father? "What made you pick being a social worker?"

"I like helping people, but I couldn't see becoming a teacher. That's not me. I guess you could say I stumbled upon it. But enough about me. Has something happened in Houston? You seem upset."

"Why is it I can't hide anything from you?" Dominic smiled.

"Probably because I've been trained to detect problems. Sometimes people aren't forthcoming, and I have to be able to read what they aren't saying to give them the assistance they need."

"It's not like you won't hear about it by tonight. The rebel forces have invaded San Pedro, the capital of Costa Sierra." Anger churned in his gut. He cared about the people in Costa Sierra and hated that this was happening to them.

"Is that where your factory is?"

He nodded. "The rebels have set my factory on fire. Most of the people were gone and the ones who were in the building got out unhurt. But the place is going up in flames. Samuel thought they could salvage one area."

"Will that help any?"

"Not really. Whether I wanted to or not, that factory has been shut down—months earlier than planned. I've asked Samuel to get the rest of my American employees out of the country. There weren't many, but I don't want a repeat of what happened a couple of weeks ago. I can't rest until I hear they're back on U.S. soil."

"So what do you have to do next?"

"Nothing in Costa Sierra. Here, a lot. I need to find a new factory location this week and begin construction as quickly as possible. My other factories can take over some of the Costa Sierra production for a while, but not for more than a few months."

She clasped his arm. "I'm so sorry this is happening right now."

The heat of her touch messed with his mind. He needed to focus on the situation with the factory, not Abbey and her effect on him when he let down his guard. He tried to push the sensations zipping through him from the feel of her fingers on his arm. But he couldn't. He stared at her perfect mouth. He wanted to kiss her. She was a compassionate, attractive woman.

Abbey scrunched her forehead. "Dominic?"

Maybe if he finally kissed her, he could move on. Then he could face his work problems without being distracted by her. He stepped even closer. She didn't move away but tilted her chin up and looked him in the eye while her hand slid away from his arm.

Inches away, her breath whispered against his lips, heightening his awareness of her. Her lilac scent washed over him and brought a calm he hadn't felt for a while. He bridged the short distance between them and settled his mouth on hers. He put his arms around her and brought her closer. The feel of her in his embrace felt so right.

Then, as though she'd had second thoughts, she leaned back, her large chocolate-brown eyes staring into his, as if delving into the reason behind what he had done. He didn't have one, other than he'd wanted to forget the rest of the world for a short time. But kissing her wasn't something he should do again. It sent all the wrong signals to her, and he didn't want to do that. So why couldn't he control himself for a few more hours, because after today they probably wouldn't see each other a lot? His life would be centered around work and Madi.

"We probably shouldn't. Madi will be waking up soon." Abbey threw a glance over her shoulder at his sister.

"You're right. I have enough to deal with." He released her from his embrace. He needed space between them before he forgot the wisdom in her words.

"Me, too. I talked with my dad after church today, and he thinks I should go forward with plans to train therapy dogs first, then later add in service dogs. He's got a few connections and will let me know what I need to get started. It'll probably be small at first, and then if there's a need I'll expand later. I may be able to work part-time at the hospital after I get Caring Canines started. That way I'll have some money coming in to pay the bills. There are so many plans and…" Her chatter came to a halt, and her cheeks reddened. She brushed her hair behind her ears, something he'd noticed she did when nervous.

"I think you should go for it. If you set up a foundation, you can take donations. I'd be the first person to donate. I can't say enough about Cottonball and Gabe."

"And we'll both be too busy for…" Again her voice trailed off into the silence, and her blush deepened. "I'm not doing a good job explaining why us kissing probably isn't too good an idea."

"I know. It won't lead anywhere, so why do it, right?" Saying it out loud didn't make him feel any better.

"Exactly. The breakup of my marriage was very hard on me at a difficult time in my life."

"Why do things fall apart at the worst possible time?"

"Is there ever a good time?"

Tired of being reminded of what he should do but couldn't, he hiked one corner of his mouth up. "Probably not. You haven't heard of any place big enough to build a factory for sale in the area in Cimarron City, have you?"

"No, but then I haven't been looking for that kind of space."

"Nothing like a deadline to get you to start looking."

"I still think your ranch would be a good place. It isn't too far outside town. Do you have any land that you aren't using for the cattle and horses?"

"I know you suggested that, but I don't know about building it here." Dominic scanned the field before him. He hadn't thought about that.

"I guess it isn't really a good idea. This ranch has

been in your family for generations, and putting a factory on part of it probably isn't what your father envisioned when he left it to you."

Dominic plowed his fingers through his hair. "This ranch has thousands of acres and not all of them are being used, but to put a factory on it?" He tried to picture it in his mind, and all he thought about was his father's reaction if he did. "But you've given me something to think about if I can't find anything in the area for a reasonable amount of money. The bottom line, the factory doesn't have to be in Cimarron City if a better place can be found quickly."

Abbey glanced toward the elm tree. "I see Madi is waking up." When she returned her gaze to him, sympathy showed in her eyes. "This will work out in the end. You'll find the perfect place, your employees will be safe, and your sister will be all right."

"I wish I had your faith." He strolled toward Madi with Abbey next to him.

"You can. You just have to put your trust in the Lord. He knows what is best for each one of us."

If only it were that easy. He'd spent most of his life trying to control what happened to him and his surroundings. Only recently was he realizing he really had no control over what occurred. But could he give up a lifelong habit and trust the Lord totally?

Abbey held two leashes with Gabe on one. On the other was Ginger, her small dog that had probably about five different breeds in her pedigree, the most obvious being poodle and Yorkie.

Mrs. Rosen stepped into her path, facing her as

though she were going to war, her fists at her sides, her stance rigid with her feet braced apart. "You've won."

"What have I won?" Abbey asked, observing the older woman grow even tenser.

"I can't have the whole east wing of Shady Oaks getting heatstroke in July. You can use the rec room, but the dogs you bring must stay in there. You can come in the side door and go right to the room. No visiting patients' rooms with the animals." You need to schedule the visits with the activity coordinator. She uses that room a lot during the day. We do have a full schedule of activities our residents can participate in. We don't leave them in their rooms all day. We get them involved."

"And that's why I think Shady Oaks is a good choice for patients leaving the Cimarron City Hospital who still need some kind of care they can't get at their home."

"But…but you insinuated Shady Oaks wasn't a good place. You got the families of the residents…" Mrs. Rosen sputtered to a stop, fury on her face.

"I didn't get the families involved. The residents did. Other than that woman last week who I told to talk to you, I haven't spoken to any other family members." Abbey smiled, hoping somehow she could mend this rift between Mrs. Rosen and her. Every time she'd come to the nursing home, the number of residents who wanted to see the dogs had doubled. Today it had looked like she had a whole wing out in the courtyard. She'd decided to bring Corky next time and hope that Mrs. Rosen would allow three dogs. She looked directly into the director's eyes. "I'm sorry if I've made things difficult for you. My intention was to give something to these residents to look forward to."

"It's easy to say you're sorry now. You've won.

You've gotten your way. The corporate office told me to cooperate with you and your dogs. It seems someone sent them a whole bunch of literature on the benefits of dog therapy, then several family members followed up with phone calls."

Abbey tapped her chest. "I didn't. The only literature I sent to anyone was you."

Mrs. Rosen harrumphed. "Just keep them in the rec room." Then she stormed down the corridor.

Abbey was thrilled the residents would enjoy her dogs during the summer indoors with air-conditioning, but maybe she hadn't handled it the best way she could. Sometimes she didn't think before she acted. She wanted to use the success at Shady Oaks to expand to other nursing homes. Emma Langford had agreed to help her with the training as well as the Caring Canines Foundation.

As Mrs. Rosen disappeared around the corner, Abbey released a long sigh and made her way to her yellow VW Beetle. She needed to drop Gabe at the ranch for Madi, then see a lawyer her dad knew about drawing up the paperwork for the foundation.

She'd never seen her father so excited. It was Thursday, only four days after she'd mentioned it to him, and he'd hooked her up with Mr. Franklin, an attorney. Her own excitement was building each day as she thought of Caring Canines' possibilities.

By the time she reached the ranch, she had an hour and twenty minutes before her appointment with Mr. Franklin. Since Sunday, the last time she'd seen Dominic, she'd been here each day to pick up Gabe in the morning and bring him back in the afternoon. She usually didn't have a lot of time to visit with Madi, but today she could stay for at least an hour.

With both dogs on a leash, Abbey rang the doorbell, and she heard Madi shout, "I'll get it."

When the little girl opened the door while maneuvering her wheelchair, Mrs. Ponder appeared in the foyer.

"Oh, good, it's you. She's been waiting all afternoon since Greta finished working with her on her exercises." Mrs. Ponder turned and headed back toward the kitchen.

"You haven't been in the foyer the whole time, have you?"

"I was throwing the ball for Cottonball. She likes it as much as Gabe." Madi patted her thigh and the bichon jumped into her lap, holding a ball in her mouth. She dropped it for the child to throw again.

"You know if you throw it, Gabe is going to chase it, too. I don't think Mrs. Ponder wants him chasing a ball in the house. Let's go out back. I have some time before I meet the lawyer."

"Great. Dominic should be home soon. You'll get to see him. He went to look at some more properties today."

I'll get to see him? Why would Madi care about that? Madi hadn't seen them kissing on Sunday afternoon, had she? Every day she'd gotten a running commentary on what Dominic was doing when Madi called her to tell her about her physical therapy. "Are you still going to see the doctor tomorrow?"

"Yep. In the morning. I'll let you know what he says. I want to walk by the time school starts in eight weeks." Madi turned her wheelchair and made her way toward the back door. "I went to the barn today to see Spice again by myself. Well, Cottonball was with me, and

Dominic was watching from the house. But I did it and got to see my horse. By myself."

"That's great." Abbey followed the child outside and down the ramp to the yard, then released Gabe and Ginger from their leashes. Even though she and Mrs. Ponder had reached an understanding about the dogs, she was especially careful that none of them ran wild through the house.

Madi threw the ball, the distance it went increasing each day as she built up her arm muscles.

"Before long they'll have to chase it in the field." Abbey pulled up a chair from the pool area. "It feels good to sit."

"I hate sitting. That's all I do." The corners of the child's mouth tugged down. "I wish I could walk now. And ride Spice."

"Don't forget to see what the doctor says about that tomorrow."

"I had Dominic put it down on his list of questions he had for the doctor. I got to brush Spice today. At least as much as I could reach. Chad helped me."

After Gabe brought the ball back, Abbey held him while Madi tossed it for the two smaller dogs. "Mrs. Rosen is going to let the dogs inside in the rec room."

"They really liked Cottonball. Maybe I should take her. If you're going on Saturday, Dominic and me can meet you there. How about that?"

"That's nice. Some of the residents asked about Cottonball, but I can come pick you up. You don't need to have Dominic—"

"And all of us fit in the car?"

"True. Maybe I can borrow Dad's van. Plenty of room in it."

The sound of the back door closing drew Madi's attention. "Dominic. You're home." She beamed. "Abbey and me were talking about going to the nursing home on Saturday. I think we should pick her up since our car is bigger. What do you think?"

Abbey noticed the dark circles under Dominic's eyes. She quickly said, "I can get my dad's van. I imagine you have work to do."

Madi pouted as she said, "Please. You've been working so much this week. Go with us."

"Listen, if you two need to spend some time together, you and I can go to the nursing home another day, Madi." Abbey couldn't forget the kiss he'd given her on Sunday. She'd even dreamed about kissing him again. She didn't like where her thoughts were going. Right now she wanted to brush a wayward strand of his hair from his forehead, to smooth away the tired lines on his face. She could tell he was working too much.

Dominic dragged a chair near them. "Madi, I don't know if I—"

"Please, Dominic. They miss Cottonball at the nursing home." Madi's eyebrows dipped down.

Dominic sent Abbey a "help me" look, but she didn't know what to say. She finally shrugged her shoulders in answer.

"Okay," he said. "But we'll have to go in the afternoon. I have one last appointment with a Realtor on Saturday morning." His chest rose and fell with a deep breath as he relaxed back in the chair.

"You haven't found anything that will work?" Abbey asked, wanting to help but feeling helpless to do so.

"No for various reasons, but mostly we need more land than is available at the sites I've been shown. If we're hiring hundreds of people, we need a place where they can park."

"We've got lots of land here." Madi held Cottonball in her lap and then gave the other dog, Ginger, a chance to retrieve the ball.

"I know, but…"

Madi's expression brightened as though she'd just thought of something. "That way we can stay here. I don't want to move."

"I haven't said anything about moving."

"I heard Mrs. Ponder talking to Uncle Chad about what you were going to do once I'm better."

Dominic frowned. "Have you been worrying about that?"

His sister nodded. "This is my home. Yours, too."

"Is that why you've been having bad dreams?" Dominic leaned forward, nothing relaxed about his posture now. "You'll think we'll move from the ranch after you recover?"

Chapter Nine

Uncertainty in a child's life could cause bad dreams, but Abbey didn't think that was what Madi's nightmares were about. It was tied to the wreck.

"No. I just heard Mrs. Ponder and Uncle Chad talking a couple of days ago. I thought we would stay here forever," Madi whispered.

He took his sister's hand. "Whatever we do will be together as a family. You'll be part of the decision. I'll think about the ranch. Abbey mentioned—" he slanted a glance toward Abbey "—that very thing on Sunday. But I'm not sure I should. This ranch was my dad's."

"It's yours now." Madi's eyes glistened.

"It's *ours*." He squeezed his sister's hand, then released it and sat back in his chair. "I'll take a look at the ranch tomorrow and talk with Chad about what he thinks. He's been here a long time and was Dad's good friend."

Madi grinned, hugging Cottonball against her chest.

In the silence that followed Abbey rose and whistled. Ginger trotted toward her, and she hooked the mutt's leash on her collar. "I have to take Gabe back to the house and get to Mr. Franklin's office. I'll call the nursing home and make sure Saturday afternoon is all right and let you two know." She started to circle around to the front where her car was parked.

Only a few yards away from Madi, Dominic caught up with her. "I'll see you out."

She began to tell him he didn't have to, but his look—as if he needed to talk to her without Madi around—stopped her. "Are you really going to seriously consider using the ranch?"

"I'll know more after talking with Samuel tonight and Chad tomorrow. I'll need to tour the ranch. It's been a while. I haven't had much of a chance since I came home to take care of Madi. Now I need to. I'll also have my lawyer looking into the zoning issues. Most of the property I've looked at has already been zoned for a factory."

"So it isn't simple."

"Simple. I've forgotten what that's like. My life seems to get more complicated by the minute."

"I know what you mean. I'm going ahead with the idea of creating a foundation. I'll start slow and see where it takes me." Abbey halted next to her car and opened the door for Ginger to jump inside.

"I'm not sure why Madi wants me to go on Saturday with you, but I'll try. I haven't been able to spend as much time with her."

"And I feel bad about not being able to, either. I do think it will be good for her to go to the nursing home. It gives her a chance to help others. Even when you're struggling, that can be a good thing. Will you two be going to church or do you want me to take Madi?"

He blew out a long breath. "I'm taking her. I don't

want to back out of something I've already told her I
would. Can we sit with you?"

"Of course. See you Saturday." She slipped behind
the steering wheel and turned on the engine.

As she drove away, her teeth nibbled her lower lip.
She was worried about Dominic. He was juggling so
much trying to meet everyone's needs. She'd been in
that position before when Lisa was sick, and she'd
crashed and burned when her life fell apart. At least
she had the Lord to turn to, but although Dominic believed in God, He wasn't really in Dominic's life.

Lord, please show him the way back to You.

Dominic came up to Abbey in the middle of the
circle of residents at Shady Oaks on Saturday. "I gave
Corky to Mrs. Parks."

"Great. Now if I only had a couple more volunteers."

"Madi is good with the residents." Dominic watched
as his sister moved from one person to the next while
she made sure everyone had a chance with the four
dogs. "This is quite a crowd."

"I know. I need to bring more animals than even four,
or have different sessions for different wings. This is
growing faster than I imagined. Just a minute." Abbey
quickly closed the distance between her and a female
resident who was trying to tug Ginger out of the man's
hands next to her. Abbey called Gabe to occupy the
man while she gently placed the mutt into the lady's lap.

When Abbey stepped back toward Dominic, he
asked, "Where's Mr. Johnson? Isn't he the one who
started all of this?"

"Yes. The nurse's aide told me he wasn't feeling well.

I'm sneaking Gabe back to his room so Mr. Johnson can at least see him."

"Haven't you been forbidden to take your animals anywhere but the rec room?"

With a nod, Abbey slowly rotated in a circle, checking what was going on with the other dogs. "Mrs. Rosen isn't here today, and I'm worried about Mr. Johnson."

"What if the director hears about what you did? Will that jeopardize you bringing the dogs to the rec room?"

Abbey sighed. "Yes, so I guess I can't."

"Tell you what. I'll go talk to Mr. Johnson and try to get him to come down here. If not, I'll find out how he's doing and tell him you'll at least see him later." When Abbey opened her mouth—to protest probably— he added, "You need to stay here. You know how to control your dogs. I don't. What if chaos broke out? What if that woman decides to fight for another dog?" He gestured toward the lady who held Ginger at the moment. "Mrs. Rosen wouldn't be too happy. Okay, be back soon."

Dominic left the rec room and found where Mr. Johnson was staying with no problem. He knocked on the closed door. It was opened a half minute later by a nurse. "Is Mr. Johnson able to see me?"

The middle-aged woman peered over her shoulder. "I just gave him some pain medication. He tried to stand earlier today and fell. He didn't break anything, but he's been in some pain. He's not too happy he can't go to the rec room."

"Thanks. I won't stay long." Dominic moved past the nurse.

"He'll most likely fall asleep soon, which would be the best thing for him."

Dominic saw a thin man with a few tufts of gray hair on his head lying in a bed, his eyes closed. Wondering if Mr. Johnson had already gone to sleep, Dominic quietly approached him. He didn't want to disturb the man, but Dominic had seen the worry on Abbey's face as the residents had entered the rec room earlier. No doubt she was concerned about Mr. Johnson.

Mr. Johnson's eyes snapped open. "Who are you?" he asked in a weak, gravelly voice.

"I'm Dominic Winters, a friend of Abbey's. She was hoping you were all right."

"Why didn't she come herself?"

"We have four dogs in the rec room, and it's a madhouse. Everyone wants to see the dogs at the same time. I'm afraid if she left me in charge, we'd have dogs running everywhere."

The old man cackled, then started coughing, his eyes tearing. "Four dogs. I can imagine the scene. How many residents are in there?"

"Thirty."

"And four dogs?" Mr. Johnson shook his head, his eyes sliding closed then reopening. "No wonder you escaped. I would have, too."

"I understand you took some pain medication, and it might make you sleepy."

Mr. Johnson frowned. "Yes. I can feel it kicking in. Tell Abbey to come see me another time. I'll be better soon. No use—" his eyes closed "—trying to...see me...now."

When the man appeared to be asleep, Dominic backed away from the bed. But Mr. Johnson lifted his eyelids halfway and murmured, "She and Gabe saved my life. Take care of her."

Dominic stopped and waited for the man to say something else. A few minutes later, he realized Mr. Johnson truly was asleep, and Dominic hurried back to the rec room. *She saved my life.* Abbey? How had she and Gabe done that?

When he entered, the residents were sharing the animals with Madi on the right side of the circle and Abbey on the left. The four dogs were calm throughout the rest of the hour they were there. Only once did a resident want to keep Cottonball longer. Madi directed her wheelchair to the lady and called Cottonball to her. The bichon jumped from the patient's lap to Madi's. His sister then passed her dog to the next resident. The lady grumbled under her breath, but Madi smiled and thanked her for giving Cottonball to the woman sitting next to her, then backed up her wheelchair a few feet.

"She has a gift for this. I may have to solicit her help more often," Abbey whispered, close to Dominic.

"I never saw this side of my sister. The peacemaker."

"You haven't seen her a lot in normal situations. She's going to grow up to be a caring person."

"She's growing up too fast. She'll be nine in two weeks. I can't believe that."

"Oh, are you going to have a big birthday party for her?"

Dominic rubbed his nape. "I hadn't thought about that."

"All little girls her age should. I can help you if you want."

"What else am I forgetting?"

"I hope you're doing something fun for the Fourth of July. Most kids love fireworks."

"That's Thursday!"

"What do you usually do for the Fourth?"

He shifted around, facing her. "Work. Everyone is off that day, and I can get a lot done then."

Abbey laughed. "You need someone to teach you how to play."

"I have Madi."

"Yes, but playing with dolls is probably not your forte."

"You got me there. So what do you suggest for the Fourth?"

"Come over to my parents' house. They always throw a barbecue for friends and family, then we watch the fireworks. They live down the river from where they shoot them off, and we have a great view."

"I hate to intrude on family time."

"Please. My dad would probably wonder why I didn't ask you and Madi. It's very casual. There'll be a lot of kids of all ages, so Madi will have someone to play with. She needs to be around children her age more." Abbey caught sight of one of the eight men in attendance sitting between two women fighting over him. "I'd better go rescue him." Before she left, she bent toward his ear and whispered, "By the way, don't say anything to Madi about her birthday party. I want us to surprise her."

He watched her give one of the ladies Corky while she started talking to the other one. Suddenly he was committed to going to a Fourth of July celebration with Abbey and Madi, and then hosting a surprise birthday party nine days later. He should have thought of doing something for his sister's birthday, but this was all so new to him. In Houston he never had to worry about birthday parties or holidays.

And he somehow had to fit in getting the plans for

his factory off the ground. After viewing the last piece of property the Realtor had shown him this morning, he realized he had no choice; he would use Winter Haven.

He could only imagine what his father would have said if he was here. Dominic remembered when a developer had wanted to buy part of the ranch years ago. His dad had flipped out and come close to physically tossing the man off the ranch. Dominic's mother had stepped in and calmed him down, but at dinner that night his father had ranted about how important this land was to the Winters family.

Dominic shoved the guilty feelings aside. He wasn't his father, and he certainly didn't owe his dad his allegiance. Not after Susie.

Abbey, along with Gabe, entered Mr. Johnson's room on Tuesday, his leg in a cast.

Mr. Johnson gave her a smile. "Did you sneak him in after all?"

While her Lab perched himself so Mr. Johnson could touch him, Abbey answered, "I thought about it, but Mrs. Rosen and I had a long conversation this afternoon. We've set up a regular schedule with the activity coordinator to bring the dogs to the nursing home. Emma is going to do that while Mrs. Rosen is allowing me to visit the patients who would like to see the dogs but aren't able to come to the rec room. You were first on my list."

"I never thought I would see the day Mrs. Rosen would agree to this. How did you change her mind?"

"Yesterday I prayed about it, and this morning I made an appointment with the head of the hospital, a friend of Mrs. Rosen's, and explained about what I was trying to do. He'd heard good reports from the staff, so he agreed to talk with Mrs. Rosen about how Gabe has cheered up the patients at the hospital for the past few months. He called her while I was right there in his office."

Mr. Johnson's grin widened. "Girl, you did good."

"It was all God. I handed the problem over to Him yesterday and look what He did. I'd been trying to find a way on my own and not succeeding." Abbey took the chair near his bed. "How are you feeling? What happened to your leg?

"I tried to get up on my own again, and this time I broke my leg. Tell Madi I know how she feels. I think my meds make me dizzy sometimes. The doc is running some tests. You know the drill. I feel like a pincushion. But it won't be long before I'm back in the rec room. I imagine you'll need my help with some of the residents who have forgotten how to share."

"Share? This from the man who wanted to keep Gabe to himself."

His pale cheeks reddened. "Still do." Mr. Johnson rubbed behind the Lab's ears. "How's that young man who came Saturday—Madi's brother?"

"Fine, I guess. He's been busy making plans to build a factory here in Cimarron City."

"Good for him. The town could use a new employer. I like him. Are you two dating?"

Abbey blushed. "No. We're friends, because we both care about Madi."

Mr. Johnson's eyes twinkled. "You know, that little girl needs a mother. So sad she lost both of her parents. I don't mind sharing Gabe with her—or Bertha Parks.

She's got the hots for me. She's visited me every day I've been stuck in this room."

As Mr. Johnson went on about Mrs. Parks's visits, Abbey's mind drifted. Madi did need a mother. Was that why she was attracted to Dominic? Because of Madi? Her feelings about Dominic had her all confused. And worse, she still couldn't get their kiss out of her mind.

When the nurse came to give Mr. Johnson his medication, Abbey said goodbye. She needed to deliver Gabe to Winter Haven. Emma had worked with Cottonball yesterday and today, training the dog. Soon Abbey would have Gabe back home with her, but until then Madi needed him. She was still having bad dreams most nights.

As she walked to her car, she wondered if Dominic would be at the house. She hadn't seen him yesterday. But even though he wasn't there, Madi had talked nonstop about her brother and how wonderful he was. She was beginning to suspect the child was on a mission to bring Abbey and Dominic together. Was it just her imagination? Or wishful thinking?

Dominic brought his gelding to a halt on the edge of a large field that butted up against the highway into town. Samuel, who had flown in from Houston, pulled up next to him on his horse.

Dominic swept his arm across his body. "This is where we'll build the factory. This area of land is only three miles from the outskirts of town, and it has highway access. The mayor and city council assured me there will be no problem rezoning this piece of property."

Samuel nodded. "We should be able to break ground

within the month. We're taking bids from construction companies right now."

"Good. The architecture firm we've used before will be here in the morning, and we'll meet with them, then after the long weekend with the Fourth of July, I want everyone on board. I want the factory operational by fall. Let's head back to the house. We have that conference call in an hour."

Samuel pulled his reins to the right, and his mare turned toward the barn. "Thanks for humoring me. I haven't been on a horse in almost a year."

"But you've been working overtime for me, and I appreciate it, because when this factory is up and running, I intend to promote you to president of the company. I'll become the chairman of the board and still have my hand in certain aspects of Winters Clothing and Textiles."

Samuel's eyebrows shot up. "You going to take a long vacation or something?"

Dominic chuckled. "Don't say it like I've never taken a vacation."

"When did you ever take a vacation?"

"Every time I came to Winter Haven, I was on vacation."

"Could've fooled me. You were constantly working from here, much like you've been doing for the past seven months."

"Okay, I'm not taking a vacation. At least not until Madi can get around better and doesn't have to have such intense physical therapy. I'm refocusing my life. When I made the decision to use some of the land on the ranch for my factory, I decided I owed it to my father to get more involved in the rest of the ranch operations.

I'm going to trim the cattle herd and expand the horse-breeding program."

Dominic breathed in the grass-scented air as his gaze swept over the land. As far as he could see and beyond was his property. Until recently, when he'd gone out riding each evening to different areas of the ranch, he'd forgotten how much he'd once loved this place. The least he could do was honor his dad's vision. Did that mean he'd forgiven his father for falling in love with his fiancée? He definitely wasn't as upset as he once was, but he hadn't yet truly forgiven him. The bitterness had dwelled deep in his heart. These past months it had resurfaced once more, leaving him struggling to figure out what to do.

"Who's visiting?" Samuel asked as they neared the barn.

Dominic glimpsed Abbey's yellow VW Beetle. "A friend. She's been helping with Madi."

"She?"

"Stop right there. She's a friend. That's all."

"Why? Is she married?"

"No."

"Is she too old?"

"Thirty, and she's beautiful, caring and gracious."

"So what's wrong with her?"

"Not a thing," he said in a voice that came out harsher than he intended.

Samuel's eyebrows went up again.

"It's me. I'm not ready."

"Why not? We've been friends since college, and I saw how you were after Susie left you. Don't you think eleven years is long enough?"

"I was totally wrong about Susie. Never in my wildest dreams did I think she would fall in love with my dad and that he would return those feelings."

"I know betrayal by two people close to you can hurt like nothing in this world, but you've got to let the pain and anger go. You've driven yourself for years. I think it's great that you're finally slowing down and refocusing your life. God never meant for someone to work all the time and not pause to have fun and savor what life has to offer. That's why He rested the seventh day. You've got your sister to look out for now."

"And she could use a mother? Is that what you're saying?" He'd been thinking the same thing. He wanted to try dating Abbey and see what could develop between them. But did she really care about Madi? He knew how she felt about her husband's betrayal. Would she ever be ready to open her heart again?

"Not totally. But she could sure use her older brother being here for her one hundred percent. In ten years she'll be all grown-up and heading to college. It'll be here before you know it. My kids are growing like weeds."

Dominic dismounted and began walking his horse to cool down. He glanced at the house and wondered how long Abbey would stay. Did he want to introduce her to his best friend? That would make Samuel read even more into his relationship with Abbey. And he wasn't sure he could handle that right now.

On the way to the ranch, Abbey quickly swung by the main post office to run in and mail a package. She put the windows down several inches, then hurried toward the building to drop off the box. She opened the door that read Enter at the same time her ex-husband came out of the exit one. He looked at her and kept going. In the post office she glanced out the large plate-glass window and spied Peter meeting his very pregnant wife on the sidewalk coming from the direction of the drugstore. He leaned toward her and kissed her.

Abbey froze. She'd known his wife was going to have a baby, but this was the first time she had seen her while she was pregnant. A cold knife stabbed her, and for a moment what happened three years ago between Peter and her deluged her all over again.

Abbey put the car in Park, staring at the ranch house. How had she driven so far without knowing it? The package she should have mailed sitting on the passenger's seat spoke to her state of mind after seeing Peter and his pregnant wife.

Mrs. Ponder stepped out onto the porch and waved. Abbey climbed from the car and walked to her, as if she were on autopilot.

"I just made some iced tea. Would you like a glass?"

"Yes, thanks." Abbey followed the housekeeper to the kitchen and sank into a chair. "Where's Madi?"

"She's still working with the physical therapist." Mrs. Ponder handed her a glass. "Are you all right?"

"I've had better days."

Wasn't that an understatement?

"That's it. No more," Madi said in a voice loud enough that Abbey heard her all the way from the physical therapy room.

Abbey rose, grateful for the distraction. "Maybe I should go in and see what's going on."

"Greta has been pushing her to do more. The child just isn't putting in the time like she should."

"Why not?" Abbey retook her seat.

"I think it's because her brother is gone a lot and she's here either doing her makeup schoolwork or exercising to strengthen muscles she hasn't used much in the past months." Mrs. Ponder looked directly at Abbey, her eyebrows scrunched together. "I'm not very good with little girls. Out of experience. I'm not sure how to entertain her."

"How's Cottonball doing?"

"She spends a lot of time talking to Cottonball and sitting on the back deck watching the people working down at the barn. The dog seems to be her best friend now. She needs other children here."

"Has anyone suggested having one of her friends from school over to visit?"

"Madi doesn't want that. She'll be in a wheelchair. They won't be."

Abbey took a long sip of her drink. "I'll talk to her after Greta leaves."

"Good. She'll listen to you." Mrs. Ponder glanced at the wall clock. "Greta ought to be leaving soon."

"I'll go to the workout room and peek in."

When Abbey and Gabe checked out what was going on between Greta and Madi, the young physical therapist was zipping up her bag.

Greta hoisted it onto her shoulder. "I'll be back tomorrow and Friday. I won't be coming on the Fourth."

"Good. I need a rest." Madi folded her arms over her chest and glared at Greta. "I hate this."

Abbey stepped into the room. While Gabe trotted over to Madi, Abbey said to the child, "I heard you've been upset."

Greta nodded toward Abbey and hurried past her.

Abbey strolled farther into the room. "What's going on?"

"I hate my life."

Abbey knelt next to Madi in her wheelchair. "I know this is hard for you, but things will be so much better by fall. You'll get to go back to school, be with your friends—"

"I don't want to. Nobody wants to be with me." Tears welled into her eyes.

"Oh, baby, that's not true. I do. Dominic does." Abbey wrapped her arms around Madi.

"He won't when he finds out what I did." Wet tracks streaked down the child's face.

"Of course he will. He loves you. That kind of love doesn't go away easily."

Madi buried her face against Abbey and she mumbled, "I'm the reason the plane crashed."

Chapter Ten

I'm the reason the plane crashed. Madi's words stopped Abbey cold. Was this why the child had nightmares? "Why do you think that, Madi?"

"I wasn't supposed to bring Zoe with me on the trip, but I didn't want her to be home alone. I snuck her on the airplane."

"How did you do that?" Abbey leaned back to look at Madi, but her arms stayed loosely around the child.

"In my backpack. I kept it unzipped partway so she could breathe. But she started barking. When I opened the bag, she jumped out and into my dad's lap. It must have scared him. After that, everything went wrong. Dad slumped over." Tears poured from her eyes. "Mom was yelling. The plane was going down. I didn't mean it. I…" Her voice choked on a sob.

Abbey held Madi against her. "It wasn't your fault. Your dad had a heart attack. That happens. It wasn't because he was scared when Zoe jumped into his lap."

"I'm sorry I wanted Zoe to go to Padre Island with me. I shouldn't have disobeyed Mom. I'm the…"

Soon, Madi was sobbing so hard Abbey could hardly

tell what she was saying. She strengthened her hold on Madi, hoping to convey her support and love. This child had become so important to her in less than a month.

"What happened?" Dominic's voice sounded above the sobbing.

Abbey looked over her shoulder at Dominic, who strode toward them with another man right behind him. "Madi thinks she caused the plane crash. I'm trying to reassure her she didn't."

"Of course you didn't." Dominic knelt next to Abbey and took his sister from her embrace. "Honey, Dad had a heart attack. You didn't cause that. He knew something was wrong and was trying to find a safe place to land when it happened."

Madi pulled back. "How do you know that?"

"He radioed his location. He knew he was in trouble, and your mom didn't know how to fly the plane."

"She was freaking out. I'd been asleep and woke up when she was talking loudly. That's when Zoe started barking."

Poor child. Abbey could only imagine the chaos that happened so quickly. Thinking she'd killed her parents and dog. No wonder she had nightmares. She laid her hand on Madi's back. "There's no way you did anything wrong. Things happen that we can't control sometimes, and there is nothing we can do."

"Abbey is right, honey. No one was to blame. It was an accident." Dominic scooped Madi into his arms. "C'mon. I'm taking you upstairs. You didn't sleep very well last night. Rest and we'll talk later."

Her eyes shining with tears, Madi placed her head on Dominic's shoulder. "I need Cottonball and Gabe."

"I'm bringing them," Abbey said, and gathered up Cottonball and signaled for Gabe to follow.

As she mounted the stairs behind Dominic, she peered back at the man standing in the foyer watching them. That must be Samuel Dearborn. Dominic said he was going to visit. She knew the man was a good friend, more than an employee. She was glad he was here, because Dominic needed a friend he could talk to. Dominic was keeping something from her that she hoped he would at least share with Samuel.

In the child's room, Dominic settled her on her bed and sat down next to Madi. "I'm staying right here until you fall asleep. See, Cottonball and Gabe are here, too."

Abbey set Cottonball on the covers while Gabe jumped up beside Madi. Then Abbey backed away, wanting to give sister and brother some alone time. As she left, Madi's eyelids slid close slowly.

Abbey realized how much she loved the child. She also discovered that she loved Dominic, too. But were those feelings because of Madi? Had his kiss the other day been in gratitude for what she was doing for his sister? She could never settle for anything less than all of a man. She had done so with her husband, and their marriage had fallen apart with their first real test.

At the bottom of the staircase, the tall thin man with a bright smile moved toward her. "I'm Samuel Dearborn. You must be Abbey Harris."

She shook his hand. "Yes. Dominic may be a while. He's trying to get Madi to take a nap. She hasn't been sleeping well."

"Not to mention she had an operation a few weeks ago."

"Yes, she's been through a lot."

"I really appreciate you helping Dominic with her. It's been hard on him, especially with all that has been going on at the company."

"Madi is special. It's easy to love her." The sounds of the child's heartache a few moments ago echoed through Abbey's mind. A pressure in her chest expanded, making it difficult to breathe.

"When she visited Dominic in Houston, my daughter and her were inseparable. We all went to Padre Island for a four-day weekend."

"So Dominic *has* taken a few days off for a vacation."

"Not technically. He still conducted business at the beach or the pool."

Abbey laughed. "That sounds like the man I've gotten to know."

Samuel peered over her shoulder. "Shh. We need to quit talking about him before he demands to know what we said," he whispered loud enough for anyone nearby to hear.

Dominic's laugh floated to Abbey as she turned toward him. "She must have fallen asleep fast."

"About a minute after you left. I waited a while to make sure she didn't wake back up. I hope this guy hasn't been telling you any deep, dark secrets about me."

"Oh, that must mean there are deep, dark secrets for me to uncover."

For a few seconds Dominic's expression showed concern, as though there was something he wanted kept from her. And she got the feeling Samuel knew what it was. Then Dominic's features morphed into a neutral facade.

She forced a smile. "I'd better go. Walk me out, Dominic."

"Sure."

Out on the front deck she paused and faced him. "I don't know what you overheard with Madi, but she thought bringing Zoe on the plane when she wasn't supposed to caused the crash." Abbey went on to tell him the gist of their conversation before Madi broke down.

"I told her the crash was caused by Dad having a heart attack."

"She thought Zoe surprising your parents caused it, and I believe that's what is behind her nightmares."

"I agree. Poor kid. I wish she had told me."

"I hope she'll have fewer now as realization sinks in that it was an accident."

"I'll be reassuring her every chance I get."

"Good." She started down the steps.

"What time do you want us to come on Thursday to your parents'?"

"The party starts at five."

"Can I bring anything?"

"Only you and Madi and the list of her friends from school. I've already started making birthday plans."

"What kind of plans?"

"A surprise for her and you. You might let something slip, so you'll just have to wait like Madi."

"How much do you think you'll need to buy everything?" Dominic dug into his back pocket and removed his wallet.

"Put that away. Part of it is my treat and the other half you can pay for after the party."

His jaw firmed. "But—"

She held up her hand. "Stop, or I won't do it. We're either a team in this or you can go solo."

His eyes narrowed on her face. "As a team member, I should really know how much you're spending and what you're planning."

"You really don't like surprises."

"Not one bit. I've learned surprises can be devastating."

She tossed him a grin over her shoulder and strolled toward her car. "Well, not this one. See you Thursday."

She felt the drill of his gaze as she climbed into her car. It thrilled her to the core, which only reinforced how much she had started to care about Dominic.

That was a good thing, right?

"Emma, I'm so glad you could make it. Come on in. Dad and Mom are out back. How did it go yesterday with Cottonball?" Abbey asked, stepping to the side to let her friend and her ten-year-old son, Josh, into her parents' house.

"Great. I think she knows all she should. Dominic told me yesterday that Madi didn't have one nightmare Tuesday night." Emma put her hand on her son's shoulder to keep him still.

"She didn't? That's wonderful. I hope last night went as well."

"Mom, can I go out back?" Josh asked, shrugging out of her hold.

"Yes, but remember to behave. No firecrackers."

As Josh darted toward the back of the house, Abbey asked, "What's this about firecrackers?"

"I found him and the neighbor boy blowing up anything they could with some firecrackers earlier today.

He doesn't know what the word *danger* means. He'll try anything. What happened to his uncle in the army hasn't slowed him down one bit. His antics have given me a few gray hairs and I'm only thirty-one." Emma frowned. "I need to put this morning behind me. Tell me some good news. How's the paperwork for the foundation coming along?"

"Almost done. In the meantime, I think we should start looking at training a few more dogs. Dad said we could use the animal hospital for now until we grow bigger."

"The weekends would be a good time to do that."

The doorbell rang. "I'll talk with you later about setting up a schedule and looking for the kind of dogs that will work best." Then Abbey went to let the guests in.

When she opened the door, she found Dominic and Madi waiting, with Gabe next to them.

"Sorry we're late. We decided at the last minute to bring Gabe." Dominic held the screen door open while Madi maneuvered her electric wheelchair over the slight hump and into the house.

The child grinned. "I didn't have a bad dream for two nights. I know how much you love Gabe and miss him."

"We thought Cottonball is ready to go solo, so that Gabe can go home." Dominic held Abbey's gaze.

"That's what Emma told me a few minutes ago. I'm so glad that Cottonball is ready. She's a smart dog."

"Yep, that's my dog." Madi sat up straighter with her chest thrust out. "Is Emma here?"

"Out back. We put up a temporary ramp from the door to the patio, like out front. You should be able to get around with little or no trouble."

"Thanks." Madi headed for the back with Gabe trotting next to her.

"She was up at the crack of dawn ready to come over." Dominic snagged Abbey's gaze. "It was her idea to let Gabe go home. She thought he was missing Corky and Ginger."

"It's more likely they're missing Gabe. How did everything go yesterday with your plans for the factory?"

"Moving right along. I'm actually getting excited about the possibilities of the factory being here in Cimarron City. I know the mayor is thrilled. He's pushing the zoning through as fast as he can. We should break ground by the end of the month."

"It sounds like things are starting to settle down for you. Have you decided to stay in Cimarron City?"

"Yes, for the time being. I'm going to make some changes around the ranch after I get the factory taken care of."

"What kind of changes?"

As Dominic told her about shifting the focus of Winter Haven from cattle to raising horses, she saw the excitement spark his eyes. Before she could ask him any questions about his decisions, her father came into the foyer.

"I'm Wes Harris." Her dad shook Dominic's hand. "I'm glad we could finally meet."

"I want to thank you for giving my sister a tour of your animal hospital. She talked about it for days."

"Anytime Madi wants to visit, she can. I saw her outside and wondered what was keeping you two. All the fun is happening out in the backyard." Her dad glanced at Abbey. "Your mom has gathered the kids to play a game, and she could use your help. There are more here this year than usual."

"I'll help, too. That's the least I can do for being invited this evening," Dominic said.

Outside, her parents' piece of property stretched toward the woods on one side and the river on the other. Her father's dogs and Gabe mingled among the guests, a lot of them from the neighborhood. "Mom and Dad have the best view of the fireworks, so everyone gathers here to watch. And my parents go all out."

"I see what you mean. A big waterslide and a bouncy house." Dominic stood next to Abbey and took it all in, while her father left to start grilling the hamburgers and hot dogs.

"Mom's a firm believer that a child who is kept occupied stays out of trouble. And there are activities for the ones who don't want to jump around or get wet." Abbey pointed toward the fenced-off area with a petting zoo. "She calls in a few favors and always has some unusual animals as well as the regular ones. I see Madi is already over there."

"Where's your mom?"

"She's setting up the turtle races."

Dominic's eyebrow hiked up. "Turtles and racing shouldn't go together in the same sentence."

"Yeah, I know. C'mon. I'll introduce you to her. We'll probably be crowd control for when the race begins."

Dominic laughed. "Never thought I would be doing something like that."

When she peered at him, the merriment in his eyes mesmerized her, and she forgot what she was going to say. Everything around her faded, except for Dominic. She didn't want to care, to love him, but it was too late.

* * *

Abbey sat in a lounge chair between Dominic and Madi, enjoying the sounds of laughter, oohs and aahs coming from the people lined up near the river to view the spectacular Fourth of July display. The last burst of fireworks splashed across the dark sky, illuminating the river in red, white and blue. Everyone applauded and cheered.

Abbey looked over to say something to Madi. Her father switched on the backyard lights now that the fireworks were over. Suddenly Madi's eyelids drifted closed.

Abbey turned toward Dominic. "Madi is asleep. I'm not surprised, considering how hard she played with her friend Brandy. I'm so glad there was someone here from her class at school."

"Me, too."

"Do you have that list for me?" Abbey whispered, in case Madi wasn't totally asleep.

"Yes." Dominic stuffed his hand into his pocket and withdrew a piece of paper. "Want something to drink?"

"Yeah, I think I'll come with you. We can still keep an eye on Madi."

Abbey grabbed a water bottle from the ice chest while Dominic snatched a soda pop. Then he moved toward the bank of the river about ten yards away from Madi, who was still sleeping.

"I'm glad there's a good breeze tonight. The mosquitoes aren't as bad." Abbey came up beside him and tipped her water to her mouth.

"Also keeps the heat bearable."

Abbey glanced at Madi. Gabe had come up to her

chair and plopped down beside it. "I think my dog is tired, too."

"Today has been a nice distraction from everything I need to do."

"Back to work for both of us tomorrow. I didn't get a chance earlier to ask you what made you decide to change cattle for horses at Winter Haven. I got the impression that you weren't interested in becoming involved with the ranch."

"So did I for a while, but as I rode over the land looking for a place to put the factory, I began to remember how much I used to love the place."

"What changed that for you?"

Dominic inhaled a deep breath, his eyebrows dipping down to form deep grooves at the bridge of his nose. His mouth tightened, and he faced the river, throwing his profile into the shadows.

Silence hovered between them, and Abbey realized this was a subject he didn't want to discuss. Why? She knew he held part of himself back from her, even after she'd told him about her husband's abandonment.

Realizing she'd overstepped their boundaries, she said, "I didn't mean to pry," and started to turn away to help her mother clean up.

Dominic caught her arm and brought her back toward him. "My father and I had a falling-out years ago, and I left home, not intending to ever come back. But Madi came along, and I began to yearn to see my little sister. But even then, Dad and I didn't really make up. We silently agreed not to talk about the past, but it was there nonetheless. Always between us. I've finally realized my anger was only hurting me, holding me back. It would be much easier if I made the ranch my home.

Madi doesn't need the upheaval of moving away. This is her home, too. I tried to put my differences with Dad behind me. When I did, the solution I've been wrestling with lately came to me."

She tried not to feel the hurt that he never had confided in her about the problem he'd been wrestling with. She felt as though he'd slammed an impregnable door in her face. Her throat swelled with emotions she fought to tamp down.

"In exchange for using part of the ranch for my factory, I'll fulfill what my father always wanted me to do—take over the ranch and run it."

"I'm glad." She wished she could be as forgiving to her ex-husband. She'd seen him the other day at the post office with his pregnant wife, and that had cut deeper than she thought it would. Her heart still cracked at the thought that he would have what she didn't—a family. "I've always been so close to my parents. They were here when I needed them the most."

"I used to think that about my father. He helped me through the death of my mother."

"So what happened that caused you two to become estranged?" She prepared herself for him not to answer her, and for a long moment he averted his gaze and stared at Madi.

Abbey had started to make some excuse to leave when finally he said in a low voice, "My father married the woman I was engaged to."

"Madi's mother?"

He nodded.

Abbey was speechless. Looking at him, she held back the impulse to put her arms around him. Something about his stiff posture warned her off.

"I know. When it happened to me years ago, I couldn't think of anything to say. All I could do was leave. I didn't talk to him for four years, then he went into the hospital with pneumonia. They weren't sure he was going to live. Mrs. Ponder called to let me know. As angry as I was at him, I didn't want him to die without saying goodbye. I knew I would regret that later."

"Then you met Madi and that changed everything."

"Yes. I even was able to have a civil relationship with my dad and Susie, for Madi's sake."

She thought of Peter with his wife. "I applaud you for being able to put aside your feelings and forgive your father."

"That sounds like you haven't been able to forgive your husband for leaving you."

"It's hard when I see him from time to time, especially with his pregnant wife."

"That's got to be hard. Seeing him like that. It was torture for me every time I came back to the ranch, seeing Susie and my dad together. After a while I became numb to my feelings."

"Each time I do see them, I think of all the children we were going to have. I wanted a large family. I…" The words clogged her throat. She was afraid to say anything further, for fear of breaking down in her parents' backyard.

"This probably wasn't the best place to have this conversation." Dominic wrapped his arms around her and pressed her against him. "It's never easy to look at our pasts and see what could have been."

His chest rose and fell beneath her cheek. His warmth surrounded her as though protecting her from harsh reality. She was scared to trust her emotions. Look what had happened with Peter. She couldn't go through that again. And yet…

She leaned back and stared up into his eyes, the shadows hiding part of his face. She lifted her hand and caressed his jaw. "We need to build new dreams."

His mouth curved up. "You're right but, like you, I'm not sure if I can trust my feelings. I've taken a beating the past months. It's been one thing after another."

"But Madi's getting better each day. It won't be long before she's walking again."

He cradled her face between his palms. "That's what I like about you. Your positive attitude. I know what you're saying will happen, but as I saw her playing and trying to fit in with the others today, I wanted it to be right now." The corner of his mouth hitched up. "I guess I'm an impatient man. I know God is working in Madi's life, but why does it have to take Him so long?"

Abbey chuckled. "That's a question I've often asked myself. That's when I figure the Lord is trying to teach me patience. I'm not the best student in the world."

He laughed, wiping away the intense moment between them. "I think you've described me perfectly."

Then, taking her by surprise, he lowered his head toward hers. His lips whispered across hers so softly she wondered if she'd imagined it. But when he pressed her even closer and claimed her mouth, there was no doubt.

She savored every second in his arms. Her heartbeat galloped like a runaway horse and she clung to him, wishing the moment could last for eternity. But the feel of a cold nose against her leg and a single bark reminded her where they were. And that was wrong.

Chapter Eleven

Dominic rushed over to find Madi thrashing around on the lounge chair where she'd fallen asleep. The child bolted up, looking around frantically. "Dominic," she cried out.

"Here I am." He sat on the chair near his sister.

"Where…" Madi's gaze landed on Abbey, standing next to Dominic. His sister twisted around and saw the house and patio. "I didn't know where I was at first. I thought I was—" she shook her head "—in the airplane, but that can't be."

"No, you're with me, and Abbey is here. We're at her parents' home. Do you remember?"

Madi nodded slowly.

"Are you okay?"

She nodded again.

Dominic rose. "We'd better go. It looks like everyone is leaving, and Madi needs her rest."

"No, I don't. I don't want to go yet. I'm not tired anymore."

"But I am. It's been a long day, and I have a lot to do tomorrow, and so do you." Dominic picked up Madi and placed her in her electric wheelchair. "Greta will be over in the morning, and the tutor in the afternoon."

"Oh, great. Schoolwork." A pout descended over Madi's features as she maneuvered her chair around and started for the patio.

Abbey smiled inwardly. "Tell you what. If you do a good job tomorrow, I'll come pick you up on Saturday and you can help me at the nursing home again. We could use Cottonball again, too."

"Cottonball loves going there. I'll have to be careful. Mrs. Parks wants to keep Cottonball all to herself."

As Abbey and Madi talked about Shady Oaks, Dominic slowed his pace and watched them interact. Abbey had a way with his sister as though they had been friends for years. Madi needed someone like Abbey in her life. But it was getting harder and harder to see Abbey and not want more from her. He thought of the kisses they had shared, and his gut clenched. She stirred something in him that he hadn't felt in years. But what were Abbey's true feelings? Was she around because of Madi or because she cared for him? Their kiss said the latter, but he'd been duped before, by Susie. Could he ever trust another woman with his heart?

Abbey looked at her car clock. She didn't have much time before she had to meet Emma at the ranch to set up the birthday party for Madi. Why couldn't she get all the items she needed on her first trip to the Super Center? Now she had to make a second trip.

Passing the stack of handheld baskets in the store, she grabbed the handle of the top one and didn't slow her pace as she headed back to the area where the eggs were.

When she came around the corner near the dairy section, she halted in front of the yogurt. There in front of the milk stood Peter, holding his newborn baby, with his wife next to him.

Peter glanced up and spied her. Saying something to Julia, he gave the baby to her and started for Abbey. Panic set in, and all she could think to do was hurry in the opposite direction.

Why did I run? Because she hadn't expected to see him, especially not with his new baby. But mostly because lately she'd been revisiting her emotions about when he'd left and Lisa had died. She didn't know what she felt anymore. Dominic's, and even Madi's, entry into her life threw her into confusion. She loved Dominic, but there were so many barriers in their way.

After a few minutes had passed, she snuck her way to the dairy section and saw that the coast was clear. Relief washed over her. She knew she had to deal with these conflicting emotions someday, but today was not the day. She had a party to throw. And she would see Dominic, who had been so busy recently that they often only glimpsed each other in passing. But today he would be there the whole afternoon. And she was looking forward to that very much.

"We have about an hour to set up before the guests arrive, then Dominic will be bringing Madi home about thirty minutes after that," Abbey said as she carried several sacks into the barn. "I'm so glad you agreed to help me, Emma. I want this to be perfect for Madi. She doesn't know that the doctor has said it's okay for her to ride with the physical therapist's direction."

"And Greta's coming today?"

"Yes. All Madi's wounds have healed, and she is

getting stronger, especially her upper body. She should be fine on a horse with some help. She's going to be so excited."

Abbey and Emma headed toward her yellow car, which was parked on the side of the barn away from the house. "It sounds like someone else is excited, too," Emma said.

"I can't wait to see the expression on her face. Ten girls are coming. Brandy had already told some of them how good Madi was getting around. I'm hoping this is the start of her getting involved with her friends again." Abbey slid the huge cake from the back of her car. "What do you think?"

Emma whistled when she glimpsed the cake decorated with chocolate icing as though it was dirt. An enclosed paddock made out of candy cane sticks and candles surrounded a pinto that looked like Spice. A banner on the candy fence said, "Happy Birthday, Madi."

"I think you've gotten more out of this than anyone. Since you've met Madi, you have changed. You're happier." Abbey had opened her mouth to protest when her friend hurriedly continued. "Not that you were moping around. This past year you've come a long way. Helping people has done wonders for you."

"Yeah, instead of focusing on my problems, I'm enjoying helping people solve theirs." Abbey put the cake down on a table she had set up in an empty stall that Chad had cleaned out for the food. "I think I'll have Chad come clean my house. This looks spotless."

"Where is the foreman?" Emma began emptying the bags of food. "I'm gonna need help with the cooler of soft drinks."

"He'll be here soon. He's dressing up in his costume."

"As what?"

"A clown."

Emma laughed. "Does he do balloon animals?"

"No, trick riding. He offered to be the entertainment."

"You seem at home here."

Abbey straightened from stuffing the empty sacks under the table and looked at Emma. "And what's that supposed to mean?"

"You care about Madi—"

"Of course."

"And Dominic. I haven't seen you like this in… I've never seen you like this."

Abbey leaned against the wall of the stall. "Meaning?"

"You're falling in love."

"With Madi, yes."

"And Dominic?"

"I don't know. I'm confused. When he kisses me—"

"Hey, you never told me he kissed you." Emma lifted her hand for Abbey to high-five it. "You're getting back in the saddle, as they say."

"A kiss doesn't mean I love him, and it certainly doesn't mean he loves me."

"You didn't see him looking at you at the barbecue last week."

"He was looking at me?"

"Yes, when you were in the petting area, he stood at the fence and watched you interact with Madi and the other kids."

A flush suffused Abbey's face. How had she missed that? "He was looking at his sister."

"No. He was looking at you."

Flustered, Abbey busied herself by taking the chips out of the bag and putting them in a bowl. "I'm mixed up and don't want to make a mistake. It would probably be best if we remained friends only."

"If you can manage that, congratulations. It's hard being around someone you're attracted to and act as if you're not."

"Sounds like you speak from experience."

"It was a long time ago."

Abbey checked her watch. "We need to hurry. The guests will be here in forty minutes, and we need to lay out the food, get the drinks, and then put up the decorations where she can't see them when she first comes into the barn."

As Abbey went about making this the perfect birthday party for Madi, she couldn't shake thoughts of Dominic from her mind. His second kiss had plagued her even more than the first one had. Emma might be right. How could she be around Dominic and pretend not to care about him?

"Since it's my birthday, I think we should go out to dinner and ask Abbey to come along," Madi said from the backseat in the SUV.

"Oh, you do, do you?" Dominic turned into the driveway that led to the ranch house.

"Yep. She's done a lot for us. She brought me Cottonball and let me borrow Gabe. You like her, don't 'cha?"

Like was too mild a word for what was happening

between him and Abbey. "Well, sure. You're right, she has been a good friend to us."

"Then you agree? Call her when we get home and ask her out."

Like a date? No, he was sure Madi didn't mean it that way. What would she know about dating? She was only nine years old.

"I know she doesn't have plans this evening."

"How?"

"I asked her yesterday when we went to see the people at Shady Oaks."

"First, I thought we would go to the barn and see Spice. You haven't gone for a couple of days with all the physical therapy you've had plus your schoolwork."

"We'll do that after you call Abbey."

He looked in the rearview mirror. "Why is this so important to you? I had Chad bring Spice in from the pasture. She'll be waiting for you."

"She can wait. You shouldn't ask someone at the last moment to go out to dinner."

He parked in front of the house and twisted around. "Where in the world did you hear that?"

"Brandy. She has an older brother who dates a girl and knows all about this."

"But this isn't a date."

"Yes, it is. We're going out to dinner," she said with intensity. "We'll go to a restaurant, and you'll pay for it."

"Okay, it's a date. Now what's this about?"

"Nothing. Dinner." Madi stared at her lap for a long moment, then opened the car door. "Let's call her now, and then we'll go to the barn."

"I thought you wanted to see Spice. You told me so at the mall."

"I do. You're not supposed to be difficult on my birthday."

Dominic climbed from the SUV, went to the back and let the electric wheelchair down from the platform attached to the car's rear. Then he went to get Madi. After she was settled, he pulled out his cell phone and punched in Abbey's number.

"Dominic, what's wrong? I saw you all driving up to the house. Everything is set down here at the barn."

He strolled a few feet away from his sister. "Would you like to go to dinner tonight?" he asked as Madi watched him.

"Tonight? It's Madi's birthday. What's this about?"

Turning his back on his sister, he lowered his voice. "Madi thought you would like to go out with us tonight."

"Well, why didn't you say that?"

"Because I think she is trying to set us up and she is staring right at me."

The whine of the electric motor came nearer to him. He glanced at Madi, who was now only two feet from him. "I'll see you at seven then," he said in a louder voice.

Abbey chuckled and disconnected.

"Well, what did she say? Why were you whispering?"

"She'll go with us. Where do you want to go?"

"To Andre's."

The most expensive restaurant in town. "How do you know about that place?"

"Dad used to take Mom there."

"You need reservations for it."

"Mrs. Ponder made some two days ago."

"What is this? A conspiracy?"

Madi swung her chair around and started for the barn. "I don't know what you're talking about."

For a few seconds he watched his sister drive away in her wheelchair, stunned that this had been planned out. What was she up to? He intended to find out. With a shake of his head, he jogged to catch up with her.

"Was that Dominic?" Emma asked as she and Abbey ducked behind a stall door.

"Yeah, he asked me to go to dinner with Madi and him tonight."

"Good. It's about time he made his move."

"It wasn't his idea. I have a feeling Madi is behind the invitation."

"Sure. It's her birthday. He wouldn't ask you out on a date on her birthday."

Abbey shot her friend a look. "Quit trying to make this into something it isn't."

Emma put her finger over her mouth. "Shh. I hear the wheelchair."

As the sound came closer, Abbey peeked through the slats of the stall door. Madi appeared in the entrance into the barn.

"Where's Chad with Spice?" The girl drove a little farther inside.

Abbey popped up with Emma following. "Surprise! Happy birthday, Madi!" She pulled the rope that held a large banner over the back double doors.

The rest of the guests jumped up and spilled out of the stalls, clapping and shouting, "Happy birthday!"

Madi's eyes widened, and her cheeks reddened. She opened her mouth, but no words came out.

"We caught Madi speechless. That's got to be a first." Brandy smiled from ear to ear.

"You threw me a surprise party," Madi finally said, tears shining in her eyes fastened on Dominic.

"With a lot of help from Abbey. My job was getting the list of guests to invite and to make sure you were away from the ranch."

"And you did a great job." Abbey came up and gave Madi a hug.

"So when he called you, you were in the barn?" Madi laughed.

"Yup."

The child scanned the area with all the streamers and banners released. She stared up at the ceiling where a net hung with brightly colored balloons in it. "I can't believe you did all of this."

"It was fun." Abbey stepped back from Madi to let her friends crowd around her. For a few seconds she thought about Lisa and how she would have enjoyed a party like this. Emotions lumped in her throat, and she turned away.

"You okay?" Dominic whispered in her ear.

"Just thinking about my daughter. She loved animals. This would have been the perfect birthday party for her."

He settled his hand on her shoulder. "I can't imagine losing a child."

She was not going to let anything stand in the way of Madi having the best birthday ever. She pushed the melancholy feelings away, then waded through the group of girls to Madi. "You think this is neat. Just wait. Everyone, let's go out into the corral behind the barn. I have a surprise."

"Another one?" Madi's grin dominated her face as she pushed her wheelchair knob to go forward.

"What is the entertainment?" Dominic asked as he strolled next to Abbey.

"First, Chad is going to do some trick riding, then the girls are all going to ride, including Madi with Greta's help, unless you say no."

"The doctor said it was okay?"

"Yes, Greta checked with him." She slid a glance toward him. "I would have said something earlier except Greta didn't talk to Madi's doctor until this morning. I wouldn't have even thought about it except yesterday Greta thought Madi was ready."

"I can't imagine a better present to give her today."

"Neither can I. Although she has a ton of gifts from her friends." Abbey pointed toward the table outside with all the presents stacked on it.

Emma opened the gate to the corral, and the girls filed inside and found seats on some benches that Chad and the hired hands brought into the enclosure.

Abbey moved to the center of the corral and whistled to get the children's attention. They all quieted down, girls sitting on each side of Madi.

"Every rodeo has a clown, so today we are going to put on our rodeo with our own rules and competition. I want to introduce Red Calhoun. He's going to show us some tricks. Then you all get your turn to ride."

Cheers went up when Chad "Red" Calhoun came into the corral riding a black horse. Thick, curly red hair stuck out from under a black cowboy hat. A large red nose rivaling Rudolph the Reindeer's almost obscured his white face and big red-lipped smile.

"Happy birthday, Madi." Chad tipped his black cowboy hat. "In my younger days I used to be a rodeo clown. For Madi I dusted off this outfit. All these tricks are not to be tried by you kids. I've had many years of training to do them."

Chad began riding his horse around the perimeter, the gelding going faster and faster. When he did a shoulder stand on the side of the horse, Abbey gasped along with all the girls.

"I never knew he could do this." Dominic joined the clapping as Chad removed his right foot from the stirrup and stood up on the left one as he kicked his right leg up into the air.

"When he said he'd do tricks, I thought it was going to be the horse pawing the ground, bowing. Things like that. Not this. I'm impressed." Abbey peered at the huge smiles on all the girls' faces.

Chad ended the show by riding around the corral standing up on the saddle, holding the reins. He brought his horse to a halt several feet from the girls, jumped from the gelding's back and took a bow. The kids rushed to him, Madi right in the middle of the group. All of them were asking questions at the same time.

Abbey walked to them, stuck her two fingers into her mouth and blew a loud whistle. The kids stopped talking and turned toward her. "Red Calhoun would love to answer your questions, but raise your hand and let him call on you."

He started with Madi. "Can I do that one day?"

Dominic's eyes grew round. "I can answer that. No."

Madi pouted. "But I'm a good rider."

"It takes years and years of practice to do what I did. Like I said, this is not something you can do without a lot of lessons and practice." Chad looked from one girl to the next as they nodded their heads.

"When do we get to ride?" Brandy asked, hopping from one foot to the other.

"Right now," Chad gestured toward the gate, where a hired hand held Spice's reins. Behind them were other men leading horses—eleven in all—into the corral.

Madi's forehead wrinkled.

Dominic made his way to her and leaned down. "You get to ride, too, with Greta's help."

His sister's face lit up. "Really?"

"Yes, the doctor said it was okay."

Madi threw her arms around his neck. "I've got the best brother ever. Thank you."

Dominic looked over his shoulder at Abbey, his eyes soft. "It was all Abbey's idea."

Abbey smiled as she joined them, while each of Madi's guests was given a horse.

Greta approached with Spice. "Are you ready to get on your horse?"

"Yes, yes!"

While Dominic and Greta set Madi on top of Spice, Abbey held the reins, stroking the mare's nose.

When Madi settled on the horse, she beamed. "I can't believe I'm on Spice." Tears ran down her face.

Abbey gave her the reins. "Before long you'll be walking again, too."

"Thank you, Abbey."

Greta strode next to Madi as she rode around the corral. The other girls cheered and encouraged her, then began following Madi and Spice.

"All these months have been worth it to see Madi's

face when she sat on Spice again." Dominic's thick voice cracked.

"I know." Love swelled inside Abbey as she watched.

Dominic clasped her hand and stepped back by the benches while the children rode around, getting used to their mounts. He swallowed hard. "Thank you. I wouldn't have thought of any of this. My idea of a birthday party would be getting a cake and singing happy birthday while she blows out the candles."

"We'll be having that, too. Later. After the games."

"You've thought of everything."

"I hope so. I want today to be perfect."

After all Madi had been through, she deserved a perfect day, Abbey thought. Feeling Dominic's hand still cradling hers was just about perfect, too.

"I can't believe that Brandy and Leah are coming over next weekend. Greta is going to be here, too. We'll get to ride again." Madi waved to Brandy as she drove away with her mom after the party. "I felt almost normal today on Spice."

"Kiddo, you are normal." Dominic ruffled his sister's hair.

"You know what I mean. Where's Abbey? I'm gonna see if she can come over and ride with us."

"How about me?"

Madi grinned. "You, too." She cuddled Cottonball against her. "I can't wait until I can do it by myself."

"Hold on there. One step at a time. And you are to do only what Greta or the doctor says."

Madi's mouth flattened out. "You worry too much."

Dominic spied Abbey and Emma coming toward them. "That's my job as your big brother."

He noticed Abbey talking to Emma. Abbey's whole face lit with her emotions, from happiness to sadness. Earlier today, he'd hated seeing that grief in her eyes when she talked about her daughter.

After saying goodbye to Emma, Abbey joined them. "Chad and the other guys are taking care of cleanup. If I baked, I would bake them a cake. Instead, I'll buy them one."

"You don't bake?" Dominic couldn't imagine there was anything she couldn't do. She'd come in and taken over his life and the ranch. She'd even won over Mrs. Ponder, who was much more civil lately.

"Not as good as a bakery, and I want the best for your ranch hands. They made everyone feel so special." Abbey's gaze fell on Madi. "What time is dinner tonight? Will I have time to go home and get this dust off me?"

Madi shifted her look from Abbey to Dominic. "Seven." Then she yawned. "I think it's going to be an early night for me. Why don't you two go to dinner without me? I'll probably go to sleep by eight."

"No, if you can't come, we can go another night," Abbey said.

Another huge yawn escaped from Madi. "Nope. The reservations were hard to get. Mrs. Ponder knows someone who works there. That's why we got one for tonight. I don't want to waste the reservation. Go without me. Really."

Dominic narrowed his eyes. "What's going on here?"

"Nothing." Madi turned her wheelchair around, then over her shoulder she continued, "I'll be upset if you don't go tonight. Remember it's my birthday and I get anything I want. And I want you to have dinner with Abbey."

Madi left them standing on the driveway watching her disappear inside the house.

Dominic shook his head. "You can't accuse my sister of being too subtle."

"Do you think she planned this from the beginning?"

Dominic locked gazes with her. "Yes. And if we don't go, she won't let me forget I told her it was her special day and she could decide what we would do."

"And she has decided. We must go to dinner together."

"Yep, so you'd better get moving. It's six. I'll be by to pick you up at six forty-five."

Abbey grinned. "You know she thinks we should be dating."

"She said that to you?"

"No, but I overheard her telling Cottonball yesterday when I was here finalizing the plans with Chad and Mrs. Ponder."

"No telling what else that dog knows. Too bad Cottonball can't talk."

"See you—" she checked her watch "—in forty minutes."

He should say something to Madi about what she was doing, but he didn't have the heart. What harm would it be for Abbey and him to go on a date? He certainly owed her for all she'd done for Madi. So technically, this wasn't really an official date.

Who are you kidding, Winters? You're crazy about Abbey. What would happen if we did start dating?

"This has been nice." Abbey scanned the elegant restaurant with the gold-and-white decor and crystal chandeliers sparkling in the light. "Things have been so hectic, it's good to stop and relax for a while."

"Especially with all that will be going on in the next few months with the ranch. Next week we'll be doing some preliminary work before construction starts," Dominic said, sipping his coffee.

"I'm exhausted just thinking of what you have to do in the months ahead."

"Yeah, but seeing Madi today on the horse gives me such hope that everything will be all right with her in time. I can't always say I felt that way."

Abbey could remember feeling hopeless right after Lisa died. It overwhelmed her and pushed her down deeper into the dark hole of her thoughts. "I'm glad it's changing for you and Madi. Time can make a huge difference."

"It's not just that. Reconnecting with the Lord has helped and I have you to thank for that. Going to church these past few weeks with you and Madi has refocused me on Him. I needed that. I think it's also helped Madi. I like the idea she'll be an assistant with the younger kids at Vacation Bible School in a couple of weeks."

"It gives her a chance to help, like at the nursing home, rather than someone helping her."

Dominic took his credit card out and put it with the bill. "I'm not the only one who's been busy. How are the plans for the foundation coming?"

"Slowly. That isn't stopping Emma and me from doing what we can without the foundation. Our plans are to start with therapy dogs and move into service dogs, too. We want to have dogs available depending on the person's need. The most important part of Caring Canines is giving everyone who needs one the opportunity to have a dog, no matter their income. Right now Emma and I are the trainers. Hopefully we'll be able to expand in the future."

Dominic said, "I didn't know you were a trainer, too."

"Yes. I haven't done much since Lisa became sick, but I'm getting back into it. Emma has been doing it for years. When she came to work for my dad, I started working with her. We're both members of the Cimarron City Dog Club. That's how I became interested in therapy dogs."

"I'm glad you did. Cottonball and Gabe have been wonderful for Madi."

Abbey remembered how Madi had been six weeks ago, the day before her final operation. When she thought of the sadness in the child's expression, she knew she had to do something to help the girl. "So am I. She's a joy to know. Has she had many nightmares this past week?"

"A few, but not as many as before, and when she does we talk about her mom and dad."

"Is that hard for you?"

Dominic glanced down at the table for a long moment, his mouth pinched together. "Yes and no. I've made my peace with Dad. I haven't with Susie."

"Why not?"

"I don't think I had much distance between us even while I was living in Houston. She was part of my family. I couldn't walk away and forget when she was always there. I pictured her living at the ranch. It was hard getting that out of my mind."

"And now?"

Dominic glanced around at the other diners. "I think

we should leave," he said in a flat tone as though they had been talking about the weather rather than his ex-fiancée.

"Sure." Abbey placed the napkin on the table and scooted her chair back. She was in love with him, but he still wasn't over Susie. She would not let another man hurt her. She needed to put space between them.

Silence accompanied them all the way to the car and halfway to Abbey's house.

At a stoplight Dominic peered at her and asked, "Have you made peace with your ex-husband?"

The question hung in the air between them.

Abbey remembered running into Peter with his wife and newborn at the Super Center earlier that morning. The pain at seeing him swamped her all over again—not because they weren't a couple anymore, but because of the hurt he had caused by his actions, especially concerning Lisa. "I'm working on it," she finally answered as he pressed on the accelerator when the light turned green.

"I never had a chance to really talk to Susie about why she did what she did. When I found out she was marrying my father, I was so angry. And now I'll never get a chance to talk to her."

"Do you really need that to forgive her?"

In the light from the streetlamps, she saw Dominic's hands tighten so much on the steering wheel that his knuckles whitened. "I don't know. I…"

"It sounds like we both have issues with our past."

He pulled into her driveway. "Where does that leave us?"

"Us?"

"Don't pretend there isn't something going on between us. We've been dancing around each other ever since we met. You've become important to me. I—"

She cut his next words off with her fingers pressed over his mouth. "Please don't. The bottom line is, I need a man who is one hundred percent in love with me. I'm not going to compete with a past love. You know who my ex-husband married?"

He took her hand in his and held it tight. "What's that got to do with us?"

"He married his high school sweetheart. A few months before we started dating, they'd broken up. Now looking back, I don't think they were ever over each other, and I won't go through that again."

"Susie is dead."

"That doesn't make any difference. Why can't you forgive her?"

"Why can't you forgive your ex-husband?" Anger sliced through his voice, striking at her.

"Because he left Lisa. I don't care about me, but I had to tell my daughter why her daddy wasn't there right before she died."

"He didn't come?"

"He came, but he was too late. His baby girl died without him because he couldn't deal with her illness. So why can't you forgive Susie?"

"Because she betrayed me."

"So did your father. But you forgave him."

Dominic sucked in a deep breath. He dropped her hand from his, and faced forward. "Good night."

She pushed open the car door and turned back toward him. The hard lines of his face attested to the intense emotions gripping him.

She hurried toward her lit porch and glanced over her

shoulder as she let herself into her house. She saw him start the car and back out of the driveway. All her animals came to greet her as if she'd been gone for weeks instead of hours. Kneeling in the foyer, she wound her arms around Gabe and drew solace from him.

This was for the best. She'd still see Madi occasionally when Dominic wasn't there. She couldn't do this, be around him, loving him like she did, and know that he didn't fully love her.

But something good had come out of their talk. She knew now that she needed to forgive Peter—and move on. Then she would be fine.

If only I can convince myself that will happen.

Chapter Twelve

Abbey entered the CPA firm that Peter worked for and approached his secretary, the same one he'd had when they were married. "Good afternoon, Mrs. Maple. How have you been?"

The middle-aged woman couldn't disguise her surprise at seeing Abbey standing before her desk. "I'm fine. How about you?"

"Doing great. I work at the hospital. Finally got my master's degree last year."

"Congratulations." Mrs. Maple dropped her glance to her computer in front of her.

"I'm here to see Peter. Is he in?"

"Yes. Is he expecting you?"

"No, but this won't take long."

"I'll let him know." Peter's secretary rose and entered his office. Thirty seconds later, she reappeared. "He says go on in."

"Thanks." At the door, she hitched her purse strap up on her shoulder and inhaled a fortifying breath, then went into the room.

Peter stood in front of his desk and moved toward her. "It's good to see you, Abbey."

"The other day I didn't get a chance to congratulate you on your new baby. I understand his name is Sean Patrick."

"Yes, as you know, after my dad."

"I'm glad you named him after your father. He was a special man."

"That he was." He turned toward a group of chairs. "Please have a seat. Catch me up on what's been going on with you."

She remained where she was and gave him the abbreviated version of her past few years, minus all the heartache over Lisa. "I'm excited about the foundation I'm starting."

"I know how you feel about animals. It's a good fit."

An uncomfortable silence descended, with Peter looking at the floor, then the door as though contemplating running away like she had at the Super Center.

Abbey cleared her throat. "I won't keep you much longer. I just wanted to tell you that I forgive you for leaving Lisa and me. You have your reasons and that's between you and God. But I don't hold anger toward you anymore. I wish you the best. Good day." She swung around to leave.

"Wait. That's it? You forgive me?"

At the door, she looked back. "Yes. We had some good times, and I refuse to dwell on the bad ones any longer."

As she walked from the building, lightness lifted her heart as though a burden she'd been carrying for years melted away. Now she could get on with her life, making plans for the Caring Canines Foundation. She wanted to help others who were going through difficult times in their lives, and it would give her life the purpose she'd been seeking for so long.

On impulse Dominic switched lanes at the last minute and turned into the cemetery where his dad and Susie were buried. He hadn't been there since the funeral months ago. He parked near their graves but remained in his SUV. Why had he come? Tired from working long hours on the factory project, then making sure he spent quality time with Madi, he tried to relax his tense muscles, but pain clenched his shoulders and neck.

It'd been two weeks since he'd seen Abbey, two weeks since she'd told him she couldn't get involved with a man unless he was willing to totally commit. And he agreed with her. After Susie, he realized he needed the same thing.

He shoved open the door and slid out of the car into the stifling heat at the end of a July in Oklahoma. It didn't stop him. He trudged toward the graves. He needed once and for all to put his past to rest. He'd fooled himself that he had when he'd thought by reestablishing a relationship with his dad for Madi's sake that was all he had to do.

He scanned the cemetery to make sure no one else was nearby, then squatted between the two graves. "Dad, I know in my heart you didn't intend to fall in love with Susie. Love doesn't always behave how you expect it to. It can come out of the blue and smack you in the head. It can turn your life upside down. I thought I knew what I wanted. But I don't. I do know I can't keep going on holding on to my anger against you. I will do right by Madi and the ranch. Thank you for entrusting those two things that meant so much to you into my hands."

Closing his eyes, Dominic dropped his head. He could remember times in the past few years when his father had tried to talk to him about what had happened. He'd always stopped him, afraid if they did talk about it, he would storm away from the ranch for good. Now he wished he'd really talked to his father about it. His father had loved Susie, and she'd been good for him.

When Dominic turned his attention to Susie's gravesite, none of the hurt or anger surfaced. It just wasn't there anymore. What good would it do to hold on to it, to keep himself from truly enjoying his life? He realized now that a marriage between Susie and him wouldn't have lasted. Breaking up with him had been painful, but less painful than a divorce.

"Thank you, Susie, for knowing when to let go of us, and for giving my father eleven years of happiness. I'll take care of your daughter as if she were my own."

Then he bowed his head and prayed. When he rose, a peace cloaked him as though his father had clasped him and told him how much he loved him. Not just his earthly father but his heavenly one.

As he made his way toward his SUV, his pace quickened. He'd told Madi he would be home by five today. She had something to show him. Twenty minutes later, he pulled up in front of the house. His sister was waiting for him on the front deck with Cottonball in her lap.

"Sorry I'm a little late." He took a chair near her manual wheelchair. "I see you're using that more."

"I'm strengthening my arms, Greta says. She likes

me using this one. I probably will except for going down to the barn."

His sister was sounding all grown-up. He'd noticed that over the past month. "Good. Building up your muscles is important. The stronger you are, the easier it will be for you to walk. What did you have to show me?"

A smile slid across Madi's face. She bent over and put Cottonball on the deck, then straightened, clasping the arms of the chair and kicking the leg rests to the side. She planted both feet on the ground. Her soft casts had come off last week, and she now wore braces to give her some support.

Dominic held his breath as his sister pushed up and stood in front of her wheelchair.

"I can stand on my own. I'm gonna be walking in no time." She eased back into her seat, her grin even wider. "And before long I won't have to wear these at all." She tapped her hand against one of the braces on her legs.

This was the first time he'd seen her in the braces. "Greta told me until you're more stable with standing and walking, you need to wear them."

"I know." Madi sighed. "I wanted to show Abbey, but she's been extra busy at work and with Caring Canines during the day. Why isn't she coming over in the evening at least?"

Probably because he was usually home by then. "Have you asked her?"

"No. I'm asking you. Everything was going good until that night you two went out to dinner on my birthday. What happened?"

"We had a lovely meal and then I took her home."

"Nothing happened?" She gave him a skeptical look.

"We're both very busy. I'm glad she's taking some time to see you."

"But not *you*." Madi's pout puckered her lips.

"I know what you were up to that evening. If Abbey and I want to date each other, we will. Until then, you keep working on learning to walk." He swiped the sweat beading on his forehead. "Wow, it has to be ninety-five or hundred degrees. I'm going inside." *And hope you drop the subject of Abbey.*

Two days later, Abbey was walking out of the hospital to head toward Shady Oaks when her cell phone rang. She answered it as she climbed into her car.

"What's up, Madi?"

"Cottonball is gone. I've looked everywhere for her." The child sobbed into the phone.

"Where's Dominic? Have you told him?"

"No. He's in a meeting. Please help me find Cottonball. Please."

"I'll be right there. Don't worry. I'm sure she hasn't gone far." Abbey hung up and drove straight to Winter Haven, Madi's sobs echoing in her ears.

Dominic rose from the table at the end of a meeting with the architect and the head of the construction company for the factory and shook both men's hands. "Thanks for your hard work getting this factory started so fast."

As the pair left his office at the ranch, Madi pushed herself into the room, tears streaking down her face. "Cottonball ran off. I can't find her anywhere."

"Where did you see her last?" He trailed her out of the office.

"Down at the barn. What if she ran away? I can't lose Cottonball." Her lower lip trembled, and her eyes shone with tears.

"I won't let that happen." He had started for the front door when the chimes echoed through the house. He hurried to answer the door, surprised to see Abbey standing before him. "What are you doing here?"

"Madi called me. Cottonball is gone. You were in a meeting. She wanted my help."

Madi wedged herself between the door frame and Dominic. "I'm so glad you're here. We're going to the barn to look for Cottonball." She rolled over the threshold and out onto the deck. "Let's go. What if a horse steps on her? Of a wolf comes around? Or—"

"Madi, that isn't going to happen." Dominic maneuvered the wheelchair down the ramp and toward the black building.

"It could. We don't know."

When they entered the barn, Madi called out to Chad at the other end. "Cottonball is gone. Can you help me search here while Dominic and Abbey look outside?"

"When was your dog down here?" Chad tipped his cowboy hat back on his head.

"A while ago. You weren't here."

Dominic snuck a glance at Abbey. Worry knitted her forehead. Then she peered at him, her eyes staying a few seconds before she returned her attention to Madi and Chad. His gut knotted. He'd missed her these past couple of weeks, even though he had been busy with work. He'd caught himself thinking about her at odd moments. He'd almost called after he visited his dad and Susie's graves, but he didn't know what to say to her.

"Cottonball might be between here and the house. We'll look there first." Abbey turned to leave.

"She'll need help." Madi nodded toward Abbey disappearing through the double doors.

Dominic backed away a few steps, something nagging him. Then he swung around and went after Abbey. Madi had acted upset in the house, tears and all. But now she seemed relaxed. As attached as his sister was to Cottonball, she should be howling. Outside he slowed his pace, stopped and watched Abbey trekking toward the backyard.

He decided to return to the barn and have a word with Madi first. When he approached the entrance, he heard Chad ask, "What's going on? You and that dog are inseparable. She wouldn't go off without you."

"I had to get them talking again. Abbey is perfect for us, but something happened between them."

"You need to tell your brother what you did. You know better."

Dominic entered the barn. "Tell me what?"

Madi fixed her gaze on him but remained silent.

"Madi, what's going on?" Dominic asked in a stern voice.

She lowered her head and stared at her lap. "Cottonball isn't missing. She's in my room at the house."

"You lied to me and Abbey. I'm disappointed in you. Next time you come to me for help looking for Cottonball, I might not believe you. Worse, Abbey drove all the way out here because she cares about you and knows how much Cottonball means to you."

Madi's shoulders slumped. "I'm sorry," she mumbled.

Dominic put his hands on his waist. "You need to tell Abbey that, then go to your room."

Madi lifted her head, chewing on her bottom lip. "Do you think she'll be mad at me?"

"You should have thought about that before you concocted this scheme."

"But you two should be together, like before my birthday."

"What Abbey and I do is none of your business."

"Yes, it is. We're family."

"Let's go find Abbey." Dominic indicated the entrance into the barn.

Abbey made a full circle in the middle of the backyard, trying to figure out where Cottonball would go. She loved Madi. Why would she leave her? To chase a squirrel or rabbit? Maybe. She kneaded the tight cords of her neck and looked toward the barn.

Where had Dominic disappeared to? Not that she wanted to see him. When she was near him, her common sense fled.

The faster she found Cottonball, the faster she could leave. She took a few steps toward the pool area, stopped and stared at the back door. If Madi and Cottonball had become separated somehow, Cottonball would go to the back door and bark until someone let her in. What if Mrs. Ponder had done so and Madi didn't know?

Abbey marched toward the house, but halfway there, she noticed Dominic and Madi heading her way. She waited, taking in Madi's scared expression and Dominic's solemn one.

"We'll find Cottonball, Madi. I won't leave until we do," Abbey said to reassure the child. She'd been doing so well. She didn't want the child to have a relapse and the nightmares to return.

"Madi has something to tell you." Grim lines sculpted Dominic's face.

Abbey's heartbeat accelerated. Had they found Cottonball hurt?

"I'm sorry, Abbey. Cottonball isn't missing. She's upstairs in my room."

Abbey folded her hands across her chest. "Then why did you call me and tell me she was gone?"

"I wanted you to come over when Dominic was here."

"I had to cancel the nursing home and disappoint a lot of folks."

Tears filled Madi's eyes. "I'm sorry I lied. I'm…"

"Going to your room," said Dominic. "And while you're there, I think you should write a letter to the residents of Shady Oaks apologizing for what you did." Dominic gripped the handles on the wheelchair and rolled Madi up the ramp and into the kitchen. At the door, he looked back at Abbey. "Please stay."

She nodded and took a chair on the back deck. No matter how hard she had worked the past few weeks, she couldn't get Dominic out of her mind. The bottom line was she loved him. Seeing him today only reinforced that.

Lord, I can't do this. See him and act like nothing ever happened between us.

The door banged closed, and she glanced toward Dominic bridging the distance between them. Nothing in his expression indicated what he was thinking. She started to stand, but he waved her back down.

"We need to talk, Abbey." He took the chair across from her.

"About Madi?"

"No, about us. I respect what you said to me two weeks ago. I understand why. But I've missed you."

Emotions she dared not feel leaped into her throat. She tried to swallow them down but couldn't.

"The past couple of weeks I've done a lot of thinking. I know I was holding myself back because I was afraid to take a risk. But not anymore. Not taking a risk on us is far worse." He clasped her hands in his. "Can we find a way for this to work? I love you, and I want to give us a chance."

Abbey cherished the feel of his hands around hers, but she wasn't sure it would work. "Have you come to terms with Susie?"

"Yes."

Hope flared in Abbey. "I did with Peter, too."

Dominic rose and tugged her to her feet. "Give me a chance to win your love."

"I can't do that."

He frowned.

Abbey quickly said, "Because I already love you. But let's give ourselves a chance to see where this goes. We can date—"

"After the last time we went out, I don't know if that's a good idea," he said with a chuckle.

She relaxed against him, his arms enveloping her. "Then we won't call it dating."

"In case Madi asks, what do we call it?"

She shrugged. "I don't think Madi will care so long as we're seeing each other."

He settled his mouth over hers. The touch of his lips made her feel as though she'd come home. As he deepened the kiss, Abbey gave her heart totally to him.

When he broke the kiss, he said, "I want to spend the rest of my life with you."

"I'm not going anywhere," she murmured, and kissed him again.

Epilogue

"I've put everything in the car, including Gabe and Cottonball. You ready to go?" Dominic asked, coming into the foyer, decorated almost as much as the living room for Christmas.

"Yes, but Madi is still upstairs getting ready. She's been fussing about looking her best for everyone." Abbey turned toward her husband, marveling at the changes that had taken place in the past five months.

He snagged her hand and drew her to him. "Good. That'll give us a few minutes to decide how best to tell her about the baby."

"I say we tell her tomorrow morning when we're opening presents. We have a lot to celebrate this year. Our first Christmas as a married couple. A baby on the way. Madi walking and doing great in school. Your factory built and running well."

"And don't forget about the Caring Canines Foundation."

"How can I? I'm going to be busy planning the training facility for the dogs."

"I hope you didn't mind me giving you your present a little early."

She laughed. "Mind? No way? The piece of land for the facility at the ranch is perfect. I can walk out of my house and go a few hundred yards to work. I have a feeling Madi will be spending a lot of time there."

Abbey caught sight of Madi at the top of the stairs, dressed in a dark green velvet dress with white stockings and black leather shoes. She slowly descended the stairs, grasping the banister. With a huge smile, she held her cane in her other hand. Only until recently had she used the stairs. Abbey's chest expanded with all the love she felt toward this little girl and the man next to her.

"What do you all think?" Madi made a circle.

Dominic put his arm around Abbey and drew her against him. "Beautiful. Both of my gals are. We'd better get going. We have to go by Shady Oaks before we go over to Abbey's parents, then on to church."

"Knowing Mr. Johnson, he'll be calling to see why we're late." Abbey placed her hand over her stomach where a new member of their family was growing.

"And we can't be late for church. I need to get there early and practice my lines with Brandy."

"We have plenty of time for all three places if we leave now." Dominic let Madi go first out the door, then snuck a quick kiss from Abbey.

"Please, you two can kiss later. We need to get going now." Madi giggled. "You would think you're newlyweds."

Dominic scooped Madi up into his arms. "We *are* still newlyweds."

Abbey hugged them both and laid her head on Dominic's shoulder, amazed at how God had healed their hearts and given each of them a second chance.

* * * * *

Dear Reader,

Healing Hearts is the first book in my Caring Canines series about service and therapy dogs. As a teacher of students with special needs, I dealt with service dogs in my classroom and saw firsthand how special these animals were. Throughout my life, various pets have brought me much pleasure and comfort. What service and therapy dogs can do is amazing. In the series I hope you'll see just how much they can change a person's life.

I love hearing from readers. You can contact me at margaretdaley@gmail.com or at 1316 S. Peoria Ave, Tulsa, OK 74120. You can also learn more about my books at www.margaretdaley.com. I have a quarterly newsletter that you can sign up for on my website.

Best wishes,

Margaret Daley

Questions for Discussion

1. Dominic's past ruled his life because he couldn't forgive his ex-fiancée for betraying him. Has something like this happened to you? How did you get past it?

2. Dominic didn't think God answered his prayers. He thought the Lord had given up on him. Have you ever thought that? What did you do?

3. Madi was depressed over yet another operation and a long recovery period. She was sick of being in a wheelchair. Have you dealt with depression? What has helped you overcome being sad and depressed?

4. Abbey lost her daughter three years before the book opens. She is still dealing with her child's death by trying not to dwell on memories of Lisa. Can you escape grief by ignoring your pain? What are some things you can do to help yourself work through your grief?

5. Abbey went through a period where she felt sorry for herself and Madi is going through the same thing. What can you do to help yourself when you're having a pity party? What can your loved ones do to help?

6. Abbey believed in the power of animals to help people when they are in pain. Do you have a pet? Have you ever felt cheered up by your pet? Has

your pet ever sensed you are hurting and tried to comfort you? Explain how.

7. Madi suffered nightmares after being in a plane crash. Did you ever suffer from recurring nightmares? Why? What did you do to stop them?

8. Dominic knew something was missing from his life because his work didn't bring him the joy it did when he first started building his company. Has this ever happened to you? What did you do to change it?

9. Dominic felt pulled in two directions. He needed to be in Oklahoma with his sister and in Houston for work. Have you ever felt this way? How did you solve the problem?

10. Abbey thought it was important that the nursing home allow animals in, and she fought to make that happen. What is something you have fought for? Did it end well? What made you fight for it?

11. Abbey's ex-husband left her because he couldn't handle his daughter's serious illness. He left Abbey to do it all by herself. Have you ever had to be the sole caregiver for someone sick or gravely ill? Discuss.

COMING NEXT MONTH from Love Inspired®
AVAILABLE AUGUST 20, 2013

THE BOSS'S BRIDE
The Heart of Main Street
Brenda Minton
Gracie Wilson ran from her wedding and the man who broke her heart...straight into the arms of the man who might change her life.

A FATHER'S PROMISE
Hearts of Hartley Creek
Carolyne Aarsen
When the child she gave up for adoption shows up in town with her adoptive father, Renee must overcome her past to find true love.

NORTH COUNTRY HERO
Northern Lights
Lois Richer
It takes the tender heart of Sara Kane and her teen program to make a wounded former soldier see that home is where he belongs.

FALLING FOR THE LAWMAN
Kirkwood Lake
Ruth Logan Herne
Opposites attract when a beautiful dairy farmer who's vowed never to date a cop falls for the handsome state trooper who lives next door.

A CANYON SPRINGS COURTSHIP
Glynna Kaye
When a journalist arrives in town, will her former sweetheart resist her charms or find a second chance for love?

THE DOCTOR'S FAMILY REUNION
Mindy Obenhaus
After ten years away, Dr. Trent Lockridge hadn't counted on running into Blakely, the girl he should have married. Or the shock of finding out he has a son.

Look for these and other Love Inspired books wherever books are sold, including most bookstores, supermarkets, discount stores and drugstores.

LICNM0813

REQUEST YOUR FREE BOOKS!

2 FREE INSPIRATIONAL NOVELS
PLUS 2
FREE
MYSTERY GIFTS

Love Inspired

YES! Please send me 2 FREE Love Inspired® novels and my 2 FREE mystery gifts (gifts are worth about $10). After receiving them, if I don't wish to receive any more books, I can return the shipping statement marked "cancel." If I don't cancel, I will receive 6 brand-new novels every month and be billed just $4.74 per book in the U.S. or $5.24 per book in Canada. That's a saving of at least 21% off the cover price. It's quite a bargain! Shipping and handling is just 50¢ per book in the U.S. and 75¢ per book in Canada.* I understand that accepting the 2 free books and gifts places me under no obligation to buy anything. I can always return a shipment and cancel at any time. Even if I never buy another book, the two free books and gifts are mine to keep forever.

105/305 IDN F47Y

Name _____ (PLEASE PRINT)

Address _____ Apt. #

City _____ State/Prov. _____ Zip/Postal Code

Signature (if under 18, a parent or guardian must sign)

Mail to the **Harlequin® Reader Service:**
IN U.S.A.: P.O. Box 1867, Buffalo, NY 14240-1867
IN CANADA: P.O. Box 609, Fort Erie, Ontario L2A 5X3

**Are you a subscriber to Love Inspired books
and want to receive the larger-print edition?
Call 1-800-873-8635 or visit www.ReaderService.com.**

* Terms and prices subject to change without notice. Prices do not include applicable taxes. Sales tax applicable in N.Y. Canadian residents will be charged applicable taxes. Offer not valid in Quebec. This offer is limited to one order per household. Not valid for current subscribers to Love Inspired books. All orders subject to credit approval. Credit or debit balances in a customer's account(s) may be offset by any other outstanding balance owed by or to the customer. Please allow 4 to 6 weeks for delivery. Offer available while quantities last.

Your Privacy—The Harlequin® Reader Service is committed to protecting your privacy. Our Privacy Policy is available online at www.ReaderService.com or upon request from the Harlequin Reader Service.

We make a portion of our mailing list available to reputable third parties that offer products we believe may interest you. If you prefer that we not exchange your name with third parties, or if you wish to clarify or modify your communication preferences, please visit us at www.ReaderService.com/consumerchoice or write to us at Harlequin Reader Service Preference Service, P.O. Box 9062, Buffalo, NY 14269. Include your complete name and address.

LI13R

SPECIAL EXCERPT FROM

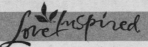

*Gracie Wilson is about to become the most famous
runaway bride in Bygones, Kansas. Can she find true
happiness? Read on for a preview of
THE BOSS'S BRIDE by Brenda Minton.
Available September 2013.*

Gracie Wilson stood in the center of a Sunday school
classroom at the Bygones Community Church. Her friend
Janie Lawson adjusted Gracie's veil and again wiped at tears.

"You look beautiful."

"Do I?" Gracie glanced in the full-length mirror that
hung on the door of the supply cabinet and suppressed a
shudder. The dress was hideous and she hadn't picked it.

"You look beautiful. And you look miserable. It's your
wedding day   you should be smiling."

Gracie smiled but she knew it was a poor attempt at best.

"Gracie, what's wrong?"

"Nothing. I'm good." She leaned her cheek against
Janie's hand on her shoulder. "Other than the fact that
you've moved one hundred miles away and I never get to
see you."

What else could she say? Everyone in Bygones, Kansas,
thought she'd landed the catch of the century. Trent
Morgan was handsome, charming and came from money.
She should be thrilled to be marrying him. Six months ago
she had been thrilled. But then she'd started to notice little
signs. She should have put the wedding on hold the moment
she noticed those signs. And when she knew for certain, she
should have put a stop to the entire thing. But she hadn't.

LIEXP0813

"Do you care if I have a few minutes alone?"

"Of course not." Janie gave her another hug. "But not too long. Your dad is outside and when I came in to check on you the seats were filling up out there."

"I just need a minute to catch my breath."

Janie smiled back at her and then the door to the classroom closed. And for the first time in days, Gracie was alone. She looked around the room with the bright yellow walls and posters from Sunday school curriculum. She stopped at the poster of David and Goliath. Her favorite. She'd love to have that kind of faith, the kind that knocked down giants.

"You almost ready, Gracie?" her dad called through the door.

"Almost."

She opened the window, just to let in fresh air. She leaned out, breathing the hint of autumn, enjoying the breeze on her face. She looked across the grassy lawn and saw...

FREEDOM.

To see if Gracie finds her happily-ever-after, pick up
THE BOSS'S BRIDE
wherever Love Inspired books are sold.

Love Inspired™

A FATHER'S PROMISE
by
CAROLYNE AARSEN

When the child she gave up for adoption shows up in
town with her adoptive father, Renee must overcome
her guilt to find true love.

Hearts OF
HARTLEY CREEK

*Available September 2013
wherever Love Inspired books are sold.*

www.LoveInspiredBooks.com

LI87836

Love Inspired
SUSPENSE
RIVETING INSPIRATIONAL ROMANCE

SEAL UNDER SIEGE
by
LIZ JOHNSON

Navy SEAL Tristan Sawyer rescued Staci Hayes, but the
missionary still isn't safe. With the bombing plot she overheard,
she and Tristan race to stop the terrorists before the naval base
goes up in smoke.

MEN OF VALOR

Available September 2013
wherever Love Inspired Suspense books are sold.

www.LoveInspiredBooks.com

LIS44554

Love Inspired

The Heart of MAIN STREET

*Available wherever
books are sold.*

www.LoveInspiredBooks.com

LICONT131BC

ISBN-13:978-0-373-87830-7

87830

0 653734 1540 0

Love Inspired®

Love's Healing Power

After surviving a tragic accident, little Madison Winters is in desperate need of comfort. And social worker Abbey Harris has the perfect solution. With the help of her cherished therapy dogs, Gabe and Cottonball, Abbey soon coaxes a smile from Madi—and her workaholic guardian. Dominic Winters is heartbreakingly handsome and is hurting just as much as Madi. But it might take more than wagging tails to get the brooding businessman to open his heart. With the help of a matchmaking little girl and two sweet dogs, Abbey and Dominic may get a second chance at love.

Caring Canines:
Loving and loyal, these dogs mend hearts.

$5.99 U.S./$6.75 CAN.

ISBN-13: 978-0-373-87830-7

50599

EAN

9 780373 878307

CATEGORY
INSPIRATIONAL

HARLEQUIN®
LOVE INSPIRED®

harlequin.com